Because You Don't Know My Name

A POTOMAC FALLS NOVELLA

K.L. HALL

B. LOVE PUBLICATIONS

Visit bit.ly/readBLP to join our mailing list for sneak peeks and release day links!

B. Love Publications - where Authors celebrate black men, black women, and black love.

To submit a manuscript for consideration, email your first three chapters to blovepublications@gmail.com with SUBMISSION as the subject.

The BLP Podcast – bit.ly/BLPUncovered

Let's connect on social media!
Facebook - B. Love Publications
Twitter - @blovepub
Instagram - @blovepublications

Because You Don't Know My Name Synopsis

Six months ago, Indigo Reid committed an unspeakable crime. A crime that, if caught, could cause her to spend the rest of her life behind bars. Attempting to avoid an orange jumpsuit, she runs, leaving behind everything, including her real name. She plans to start over in the small city of Potomac Falls before the police or anyone else uncovers her secret. When she arrives in the buzzing town saturated with its share of scandals, she quickly falls for the picturesque cascading waterfall and the promise of a peaceful, solitary existence while rebuilding her life. Although damaged by her past and gun-shy about men, Indigo finds her warmest welcome in Potomac Falls native and business owner Donovan Saintsbury. She's hesitant to pick up the pieces of her broken heart, let alone open it again, even to someone as captivating as Don.

With seductive brown eyes, a winning smile, and over six feet of cut, honey-brown muscle, Donovan "Don" Saintsbury is a masterpiece in his own right. The business-minded bachelor works hard as the only family member left in the city to oversee the operations of his family's historic diner. As the youngest of four siblings, keeping the family legacy intact has been his sole focus until he meets Indigo.

Despite the eruptive chemistry luring them closer, Indigo knows that becoming attached to a handsome stranger is risky, especially since her identity is hidden and her past is deadly. When Indigo reveals the truth about her former life, what happens when she finds out the man of her dreams is more linked to it than she imagined?

Welcome back to Potomac Falls, a small city filled with daring encounters, explosive characters, and succulent scandals.

Trigger Warning:

This book contains instances of domestic abuse and explicit language.
Reader discretion is advised.

Prologue

INDIGO REID

Six months ago.

MY HUSBAND ENZO and I had been living and breathing the same air for two years. At the inception of our whirlwind relationship, he was everything to me. He was handsome, tatted, and always said the perfect words at the ideal time. The silver-tongued devil could charm the skin off a snake and the birds from the trees. He was six years my senior and as sweet as apple pie. When we were dating, he called me in the mornings when he woke up and every night before he went to bed. His over-the-top romantic gestures, like having bouquets of long-stem roses delivered to my job, just because, or surprise weekend trips on his motorcycle, made me feel like royalty. From the moment we met, I knew I wanted to be his wife, and when he popped the question six months into our relationship, I said yes without hesitation.

Eighteen months into our marriage, everything changed. He started hanging out with a different set of friends, doing drugs, and staying out late, only to make up excuses the following day about where he'd been. It was only when he'd come home zooted on coke at three o'clock in the morning that he'd want to vent and tell me about the females he dated before me only wanting him for his money and what his family had, but whenever I would inquire more, he'd shut down or get angry. I never pressed the topic because *everyone* had secrets, and he clearly wanted to keep his buried. I knew his parents weren't around, and he never looked back when he left his hometown to move to Chicago.

On cocaine, Enzo went from loving and devoted to domineering and aggressive within seconds. Our once happy home soon turned into a house of terror, living under the same roof as him. I blamed the drugs at first and urged him to quit and get help, but his habit only worsened. Between his temper tantrums and mood changes, I always walked on eggshells, afraid of what he would say or do if I didn't. Then one night, he snapped, revealing the monster he'd always been, but I'd just been too naive to notice.

I was asleep on the couch when he pulled me to the floor by my ankles and dragged me by my hair down the hallway to our bedroom. I kicked and screamed, as he tossed me on the bed like a rag doll, climbed on top of me, and placed his large hands around my throat. My eyes bulged as I tried to gasp for air.

"Did you take it?"

"E-Enzo, p-please," I whispered, words a mere push of air as he continued to choke me.

"Answer me, bitch! Did you take it?"

My emotions were at an all-time high. I knew he had to be in another one of his coke-induced rages. I shot my gaze up to him, studying his cold, soulless eyes as he tried to strangle me to death. I scratched and clawed at his arms, using what strength I had left to try and pry his fingers from around my throat. *If I could just scream, someone would save me*, I thought. Moments before I drew in what I knew would be my last breath, I shot him the most fearless look one could give a person. I refused to die with terror in my eyes at the hands of a coward like Enzo. That was when he unexpectedly let go and fell backward off me, panting like a dog in heat.

"Man, fuck!" he yelled before punching a cereal bowl-sized hole in the wall next to my side of the bed. "Look what you made me fuckin' do!"

I shot up, gasping for as much air as possible before screaming. Enzo turned his back, and I could feel the adrenaline bursting through my veins. My eyes landed on his gun on the nightstand. The moment I put it in my hand, I knew exactly what I was going to do. It was a muscle reaction with zero thought. There was too little time to think of another alternative than the one that had presented itself. My fingertip squeezed the trigger, and I heard a click. I pulled again and again, and I listened to the shots. Enzo's two-hundred-pound muscular body hit the ground with a loud thud. I turned around so fast I almost fell over. There was a burning sensation on the soles of my feet as I ran from the bedroom, down the hall, and through the living room. I grabbed my keys and raced to my car as fast as I could.

"Come on, come on." I whimpered, frantically turning the key in the ignition.

All I could hear was the underlying kick drum of my heartbeat as the tires screeched and I pulled away.

The minute I got to a safe space, fear erupted from my body in the form of vomit. Not only had I shot my husband, but I had left him for dead. I couldn't go to jail. Pretty girls like me didn't do well in places like that. Because I was too afraid to deal with the consequences of my actions, I ran and never looked back. I left behind everything I'd brought to the relationship: pots and pans, dishes, towels, everything. With no ID, purse, or money, I stayed one night on a friend's couch before she gave me a few hundred dollars, took me to the bus station, and got me a ticket to some small city called Potomac Falls. She said she had a friend of a friend who did the hiring at a diner there. She promised the pay wasn't much, but it was something to get me out of my problematic situation.

Potomac Falls would be my reset button on life and a chance to start fresh. I could lay low and pretend to be whoever I wanted. I lifted a pair of scissors from the convenience store across the street from the bus station and cut off all my hair in the bathroom. I figured I'd get someone to fix it up and make it look good when I got some real money. I stepped on that Potomac Falls-bound bus, excited to go to a place without traps or triggers. During the twenty-six-hour-long bus ride, I blocked Enzo, deleted my profiles on all social media sites, tossed my sim card, and changed my email address. It was time to set up my new life under a new identity. I was no longer Indigo Reid. I was Neema Ellison.

One

INDIGO

Present day

IT'D BEEN three months since I started working at *A Taste of Heaven Diner* in Potomac Falls. The day I got hired, they were swamped with a charter bus full of students and parents from out of town who'd come to the city to ooh and ahh at the majestic waterfall. I could tell the hiring manager was overwhelmed by his anxious knee jumping underneath the table. The bells on the door kept ringing, cooks were yelling orders from the kitchen, and the waitresses rushed to get food and slanged hot dishes to patrons every few seconds. The lingering smell of bacon grease hung in the air as I nervously eyed the accolades and photos on the wall of famous patrons before speaking up.

"*I could start today,*" I stated, eyes shooting up to his. "*I see y'all could use the help.*"

He glanced over my shoulder, noticing the big trucks rumbling outside in the parking lot, and grunted before tossing a greasy apron my way. I breathed a quiet sigh of relief while thanking my lucky stars he didn't ask if I had a license or any other form of identification. All he did was tell me to write my hours down on paper, and we'd straighten out my payment at the end of the shift. My friend was right about the pay, but I was okay with it if I got to keep my peace of mind.

When I moved from my extended stay motel room into my studio apartment, I stayed up all night unpacking what little I had and made a pallet on the hardwood floor to sleep on. I tried my best to block it out of my brain, but for the first few months after the incident, I would cry if I traded glances with myself in the mirror. I drank whiskey and tears over ice until I was too drunk to move. Time had passed, and the seasons changed, but I was still dealing with the nightmares and waking trauma of seeing his face whenever I closed my eyes or heard a similar voice. I took public transportation to work because I was too terrified I would come out of the diner one night and find him sitting in my back seat with a gun, ready to retaliate for what I did to him. Either that, or the police, ready to take me in for my crimes.

I kept telling myself that he would've killed me if I didn't shoot him, but that only took the guilt away for a second or two. I searched the news about his death but saw nothing, heard nothing. It was as if that part of my life had never happened, but my conscience knew it did. The truth was, shooting Enzo killed off part of my soul. It was as if the moment the bullets left the chamber, I felt something inside me die. As free as I was from his aggression and abuse, I still felt chained to him and wracked with guilt. I was still waiting for the day when the flashbacks melted into distant memories that didn't feel like I was swallowing flaming hot lava. One thing was for sure: *Nothing* mattered after you pulled a trigger. I didn't wish the habit of having to look over my shoulder for the rest of my life on anyone.

Aside from the beautiful waterfall, the people I encountered at the diner were mostly polite. It only took me being there for two weeks before Donovan, the owner, caught my eye. He'd been running through my mind like a song on repeat ever since. Visually, he had everything I liked, checking off all my boxes from head to toe. Towering height? *Check.* Athletic build? *Check.* Butterscotch skin to complement his mahogany eyes? *Check, check.* A smile that could slice a girl's heart in two? *Check.* I'd only seen him in passing but was intrigued. He always looked too busy to do anything but work and breathe, so we hadn't had many one-on-one conversations. Whenever he did have a second or two to chat with me over his favorite meal, I picked up on things about him here and there and dared to say I'd developed a slight crush.

I knew it was foolish to have butterflies for my boss, and I had *no* business looking to make friends or social connections, let alone fall into a relationship. I needed to remain as distant and neutral as possible with everyone, but I'd be damned if Donovan didn't make me smile with all thirty-two teeth.

I gripped my pen and pad as tightly as possible when my palms began sweating. My feet glided over to the secluded booth in the corner where Don sat.

"Workin' hard or hardly workin'?" I asked, approaching the paper-work-filled table.

He looked up from his papers. "Huh?"

I smiled politely while gazing at the floor. "Nothing. It was a joke. Forget it. I just came over to see if you needed anything."

"What time is it?" he asked before his eyes swiveled down to his watch. "Damn, it's already past noon. I haven't eaten anything all day."

"Do you want the usual? I'm sure Tony can whip it up for you real quick. We aren't too busy right now," I suggested.

His right eyebrow lurched toward his crisp hairline. "The usual? You know my usual?"

"Steak and eggs. Cooked medium-well and sunny-side-up with A1 Sauce on the side, right?"

A wrinkle cut across his forehead. "Huh?"

I answered his confusion with a silent smile. "Just a guess." I shrugged.

"You're the best guesser I've ever met if that's the case," he responded. "I might need to pick your brain for the winning lotto numbers or something."

"If you win, you gotta promise to split it with me fifty-fifty. Deal?"

"I don't know about all that now. I gotta keep the lights on around here."

Don chuckled, and my heart fluttered wildly. He didn't smile much, although he had no reason not to show off the perfect set of porcelains he'd been blessed with. To make matters worse, everything he wore looked to have been made for no one else in the world but him. He silently let everyone around him know he didn't come to play games everywhere he went.

I bobbed my head. "Guess you're right."

"It's Neema, right?" he quizzed before I saw his eyes dart across my chest to my nametag.

"You cheated."

"I didn't! I said your name before I looked at your nametag, I swear," he emphasized.

I playfully rolled my eyes. "Yeah, okay. But yes, you're right. My name is Neema."

"Well, Neema, how about my drink?" he asked.

"Excuse me?"

"You got my food order right but didn't mention my drink."

I couldn't dare tell him the truth, which was I knew he always drank hot chocolate, even at eighty degrees outside. Telling him would make me look crazy, but I knew his routine like the back of my hand. He would always sit in the back corner, away from all the other patrons, working and watching. After plucking away at his laptop for a while, he'd order the steak and eggs special with a side of hot chocolate.

I smiled but didn't look at him. He unknowingly had given me a chance to redeem myself. "Hmm," I said, tapping my pen cap to my chin. "Coffee—black."

"Ah, nope. You almost had me there for a second. I'll take a hot chocolate," Don stated before running his hand over his head of jet-black waves.

I playfully hunched my shoulders up. "Ah, so close! Guess I can't win 'em all, huh?"

He chuckled. "Guess not."

"What's the story behind the meal?"

"Why do you think there's a story?"

"Because you own the diner and order the same meal whenever you're here and hungry. I figured there have to be other places around here where you could get the same thing."

"You're right. There's a story."

"Told you!"

"This is my family's diner, and the steak and eggs special was always my father's most requested meal, so when he died, I always vowed to keep it on the menu."

"That's nice. I like that you're still paying homage to him. I'll, uh, go ahead and put your orders in and be back with your hot chocolate soon."

"Thanks... Hey, Neema?"

"Yeah?"

"How'd you know there was a story? I know you're still kind of fresh here, but I don't know anyone here who has ever noticed or asked me about it before."

I darted my eyes over to him and smiled sweetly. "What can I say? I'm just good at reading people."

Two

❧

DONOVAN "DON" SAINTSBURY

IT WAS CLOSING TIME. I walked out of the back office and stood in the stillness of the dimly lit diner. My eyes absorbed all that was left of my family's legacy and wondered, *what do I do now?* Earlier, I'd received an email from an interested buyer with deep pockets who was looking to acquire the land and the diner on top of it to build a new luxury hotel. *A Taste of Heaven Diner* was built on my family's land, across the bridge from Seven Pines, less than ten miles from their airport. I knew a hotel would mean new jobs and more revenue for the city, but I had plans in mind for the diner. I'd been busting my ass, applying for grants and loans and trying to find angel investors to help me take my vision to the next level. The last thing on my mind was selling it, but I would be lying if I said the seven hundred and fifty thousand dollars they offered didn't make me want to reconsider.

I was the youngest of four siblings, all of which had put Potomac Falls and the death of our parents in their rearview, leaving the day-to-day operations of our family's diner on my shoulders. We weren't close like some families. I hadn't seen or spoken to my brother and one of my sisters in over five years. My other sister, Destiny, was two years older than me and lived five hours away with her girlfriend, Vanchesca. She was the only one I kept in touch with, at least bi-monthly. The immediate pain of losing my parents in a car accident had faded, but the fear that I would fail them or fuck up their life's work was chronic and subtle but always there, ready to flare up at any moment.

I paced across the checkered tile floor, past the whiteboard with the daily specials etched on it, and caught a glimpse of the parking lot through the smudged window. That was when I saw *her*. Neema was waiting at the bus stop for the last running bus of the night. I would've had to have been a blind man not to notice how beautiful she was from the moment she started working at the diner. I couldn't help but anticipate seeing her whenever she was on the schedule. Like clockwork, the bus would show up, and *she* would walk in five minutes later, clock in, put on her apron, and go to work. Neema was a natural beauty with smooth, milk chocolate skin and a timeless white smile. From a distance, I admired how her button nose was slightly upturned at the tip, the mole on her cocoa butter-kissed collarbone, and the cupid's bow at the top of her full lips. I often wondered how someone who looked as beautiful as she did, even ended up in the diner when she looked like she belonged on a runway.

I locked up before heading to my car and pulled up to the bus stop to see Neema sitting on the cracked and faded bench.

I rolled down the window. "Everything okay?" I inquired.

"I'm fine. You finally heading out?"

I dipped my chin in a nod. "Yeah. You, uh, need a ride or anything?"

She politely shook her head. "No. I'm good."

"You sure? It's no problem."

She slowly shook her head before responding again. "I said no, thank you."

It was apparent I'd freaked her out. *Fuck!* I thought. There was no way I could make it sound any less creepy, even though I knew I was coming from a good place. "No problem. When's the bus coming? I don't feel right letting you sit alone so late."

Her eyes pinged to her watch. "Another ten or fifteen minutes. Go on ahead. I promise I'm good. I'm kind of a night owl these days anyway."

"Me too. Mind if I wait with you?"

A shrug rolled over Neema's milk chocolate shoulders. "Sure, if you don't have anywhere better to be."

"Not in the next ten to fifteen minutes, I don't," I answered before killing the engine and hopping out. I took my place beside her on the bench, listening to the crickets chirping in the distance as we sat silently for a few fleeting seconds.

I gazed into her almond-shaped brown eyes, admiring how her short haircut framed her face. "So, you said you're a night owl?"

"Yeah. I don't sleep much these days."

"Oh, yeah? Why not?"

Neema swung her head in a no. "It'll sound childish if I say it, so I won't."

"You gotta tell me now."

"I can't."

"C'mon, tell me."

Air eked from her slightly parted lips before she spoke. "Sometimes I have... y'know, like, bad dreams."

"Like, nightmares?"

She ducked her chin in agreement. "Yeah."

"About what?"

"Just... stuff," she mumbled.

Even if she hadn't uttered a word, the way her eyes kept shifting from the pavement to her sneakers was telling enough.

"Y'know, growing up, my sister Paris had nightmares."

"You got siblings?" she asked.

"Three," I answered. "I'm the youngest."

"They all still live around here?"

I shook my head. "Nah. Just me these days."

"How'd she stop them? The nightmares, I mean."

"I don't know if she ever did."

She let out a soft chuckle. "I take it you two weren't thick as thieves growing up?"

I laughed alongside her. "That obvious, huh?"

"Maybe just a little."

Before I could react, my eyes caught the bus's bright headlights pulling up. "Here comes the bus now."

"Thanks for the chat," she said, standing to her feet. "See you at work tomorrow?"

"Yeah. You have yourself a good night."

She smiled with delight before gripping the metal handrail. "Yeah. You too."

I stood, watching her grab a window seat as the doors folded and the bus driver pulled off. With everything I had going on, I wasn't in the right headspace to focus on my heart, but her smile was determined to change my mind.

* * *

MY DAY STARTED with two missed calls from my sister Destiny. By the sound of her voicemail, she'd also received an email from the buyer expressing interest in buying the diner. Since the four of us were all shared owners, I knew she wanted to talk to me about it, and I was doing my best to avoid her. I spent most of the morning pouring over employee files and old financial records at my desk to find the information I needed to apply for more grants, when my phone vibrated. I turned my eyes toward the screen to see another incoming call from Destiny and rolled my eyes toward the ceiling. *This girl won't quit,* I thought as I picked up the phone.

"Yo," I answered.

"Hey, Donny."

"Hey. I'm kinda busy right now. What's up?"

"You can't take a minute to talk to your big sis?"

"I have another one, you know," I reminded her.

She smacked her lips. "We both know I'm your favorite, though. How are you? It's been a minute since we caught up."

"I'm not the one who moved five hours away to be with her girlfriend."

"You sound like a bitter bitty. Besides, you *do* know there's this thing called the phone that we're speaking on right now that allows for two-way communication?"

I sucked my teeth while cradling the phone between my shoulder and neck as I opened the file cabinet. "Whatever."

"I called you a few times earlier. Did you get a chance to listen to the voicemail I left?"

"Nah," I lied. "I told you I've been busy. What did you have to say?"

"Paris and I both got emails from a buyer who was—"

I cut her off. "Interested in buying the diner to build a luxury hotel? Yeah, yeah. I got it, too," I admitted.

"And?"

"And, what?"

"How do you feel about it?"

"I don't feel anything about it because I'm not selling."

"It's not just your decision, Donny. The four of us share equal ownership of the land and everything on it, including the diner."

"I'm aware."

"All I'm saying is, I think you should consider it. Seven hundred and fifty thousand dollars split four ways isn't a little piece of change. And besides, this could *finally* be your chance to get out of Potomac Falls and experience the rest of the world and all it has to offer."

"I'm good," I replied, hearing the frustration in my tone. "Look, I gotta get back to work, aight?"

"This conversation isn't over, D!"

"It is for now," I responded before ending the call.

It only took one email from a faceless buyer to have my sisters ready to cash in on all that was left of our family legacy. Although she didn't mention where our brother stood on the issue, I knew I would have to do whatever it took to keep my family's business afloat, even if no one in my family seemed to care but me. Before I spiraled too deep in thought, there was a knock on the door.

"Come in."

The door opened, and Neema walked in. "I heard you were back here slaving over paperwork again, so I thought you could use a hot chocolate." She placed the steaming mug of hot chocolate in front of me. "I hope you like it. I made it extra special."

I eyed her closely for a few seconds before lifting the mug. "Thank you."

She watched me take a small sip, swish it in my mouth and then swallow. "I don't know if it's because you said you made it special, but it tastes better than usual today."

"Wanna know the secret ingredient?" she inquired, voice floating on a whisper.

I leaned in with an intrigued look across my face. "Lay it on me."

"Milk *and* cream with a sprinkle of cinnamon on top."

I belted out a hearty laugh, grateful for the distraction of work and brewing family drama. "That's it, huh? That's the magic combination?"

"Yeah. Usually, Carol wants us to make it with just water. Still, as someone who occasionally enjoys a good ol' fashioned cup of hot chocolate, I thought you'd appreciate the secret VIP upgrade."

"I do. Seriously, this was just what I needed right about now."

She smiled. "Hope it helps you relax."

"I look that uptight, huh?" Neema tilted her head to the side, casting her gaze down to her feet. "It's okay. You can be honest with me," I assured her.

"I mean, a little. Okay, a lot."

"I know. Things are just a little crazy right now, that's all. I'll be straight."

"Are you trying to convince me or yourself? Because it's none of my business."

"I don't know. I think maybe I need a miracle or some divine intervention or something."

"Or maybe you'd feel better if you talked to someone about whatever's bothering you."

"Someone like you?" I inquired.

"You don't wanna talk to me. If I'm being honest, I'm a pretty mediocre listener."

Her candidness made me laugh. "Aren't you supposed to be convincing me to spill my deepest darkest secrets?"

"I don't think there's anything dark about you," she responded with a coy smile.

As soon as the words rolled off her tongue, she froze. She looked as if she wanted to curl up and sink into an invisible hole in the floor. Before I could respond, another waitress called out to her to take more orders from the lunch crowd while she went on her smoke break. "I, uh, should get back out there."

"Y-yeah. Right. Go ahead. And, uh, Neema?"

"Yeah?"

"Thanks again... for the chat and the hot chocolate."

"Anytime."

* * *

HOURS LATER, I caught up with her again just before she was about to clock out for the evening. "Neema, can I talk to you for a second?"

"Yeah. Sure, what's up?"

"I was going through some of the employee files today."

"Yeah?"

"And I noticed you don't have an ID on file."

Doubt pinched her forehead in the middle. "Are you sure?"

"Yeah. There's nothing here except for your application."

"Oh..."

"If you have it on you right now, I can scan a copy, and everything will be taken care of."

She fished inside her purse for a few seconds before popping her eyes back to mine. "Oh, shoot. I forgot I left my wallet back at my place. I woke up a little later than normal this morning and raced out of the house to avoid missing the bus and being late."

"Sure. Just bring it in tomorrow or the next time you're on the schedule."

"Uh, yeah. Sure. I'll do that."

"Where you from anyway?"

"What makes you think I'm not from around here?"

"I've lived in Potomac Falls all my life, and my first time seeing you around was when you started working here, so I knew you had to be new to the area."

"So, what you're saying is, you're just as good of a guesser and as observant as I am, huh?"

"That, and ain't too many women around here that look like you."

"I don't know if that's a compliment or..."

"It is. So, you gon' answer me or make me run through all the states until I get it right?"

She chuckled. "Texas, originally, but I move around a lot, or at least I used to," she told me.

I put my head to one side in a curious manner. "Loner, huh?"

One side of Neema's lips lifted in a soft smile. "I guess you could say I wasn't raised to plant my roots all in one place."

"You sound like a military brat."

"And you sound like you can't relate."

A quick laugh escaped my lips. "Nah, I can't. I told you, I have been here all my life. I guess I'm curious as to what brought you to Potomac Falls. You running from someone?"

Her brows lurched upward. "What? What makes you think I'm running?"

"Now who's the one that needs to relax? I'm just joking with you. Usually, people come to a place like Potomac Falls to vacation or see the waterfall, not to start their lives over."

"Who knows, maybe this place is just the fresh start I need."

"I hope it is too."

"You see yourself living here forever?"

My shoulders bounced with a shrug. "I don't have a reason to leave, never have, but I would be happy to show you around the city sometime if you're interested."

"Uh, yeah. Maybe." Neema replied as if her mind were a thousand miles away.

"Cool. Well, have a good night."

"Mmhm. You too," she mumbled while standing frozen in place.

"Is there something else on your mind?" I inquired.

She pushed out a loud sigh. "I haven't been completely honest with you."

"About what?"

"My ID. The truth is, I lost it during the move, and I've been waiting for the DMV to send me a new one, but you know how slow they can be."

"Yeah, sure."

"On top of that, I've been having trouble with my mail. Sometimes I get things. Sometimes I don't."

"That's unfortunate. Do you have another form of ID.? A passport? A social security card? Just something to prove you're you?"

She shook her head. "Not right now, but I promise I'll get it soon, no matter if I have to wait the whole day at the DMV."

"Neema, I get that, I do, but you've been working here for months undocumented, and I'm not sure how I let it go unnoticed for this long."

"So what are you saying?"

"I'm sorry, but you can't continue to work here without the proper paperwork on file." My statement noticeably bummed her, so I continued my explanation. "Look, I don't want to be the bad guy here, but there's a lot of business stuff behind the scenes that you don't know about, and I can't have any loose ends right now."

"Yeah, no. I understand."

"I don't know. Maybe I can put in a word for you elsewhere around the city once you figure out your ID situation."

Neema wagged her head from side to side. "No, it's fine. I'll figure something out. Thanks for the opportunity," she said, heading to the door.

I sighed. "Neema, wait."

"Yeah?"

"I'll give you two weeks, okay? After that, I can't help you."

She graciously bobbed her head. "Yeah, okay! I got it. Two weeks! Thank you so much! I promise you won't regret it."

Three

∽

INDIGO

Two weeks later

I WOKE up in the bathtub, screaming hysterically and drenched in sweat. It was the third time that week, which only meant one thing: The nightmares and sleepwalking were back. Tremors convulsed my ribs, and my leg bounced nervously as I sat on the edge of the toilet, waiting for the shower to heat up.

"Fuck! Fuck! Fuck!" I screamed while slamming my palm against my forehead.

It was always the same room, same bed, same menacing hands. I was always running to escape, and either the car stalled, or I dropped my keys. Whatever the scenario, I would always wake up gasping and panting when his fingertips were about to reach the handle.

A shiver cut through me as I stood underneath the warm water, praying all my fears would magically rinse down the drain. All I wanted to do was rebuild my life, brick by brick, but I'd been secretly battling with myself every second of the day. Dealing with my nightmares was one thing, but the sleepwalking was new. Two nights prior, I woke up standing in the middle of the kitchen with a knife. The night before that, it was in the living room where I stubbed my toe. I was slowly losing my mind. That, or the guilt was eating me alive from the inside out.

After stepping out of the shower and drying off, I looked outside to see the sun rising and decided to catch the bus and head to the diner early. The bell dinged against the glass door as I made my way inside. The stool at the long counter creaked as I sat, writing the daily specials on the whiteboard while the coffee maker warmed up. After that, I went to each booth, refilling the condiment bottles, salt and pepper shakers, and sugar packets.

"I thought I heard someone out here," Don said, coming from the back office. "You're in early."

My shoulders twitched. "Couldn't sleep."

"Those bad dreams again?"

"Something like that."

"You been to Edgewater Falls yet?"

"No. Only saw it from afar. Not up close," I answered, wiping a sticky spot on the counter before wiping the greasy fingerprints off the laminated menus.

"There's a nice hiking trail around there, too, if you're into that kinda stuff. Sometimes I go there when I have a lot on my mind."

"Does it help?"

His broad shoulders rose and fell. "Sometimes."

"Maybe I'll check it out then."

"We also have this pretty dope movie theater downtown with reclining seats and all that."

I snickered. "Who are you, the president of the welcoming committee?"

"Something like that." He mocked me with a smirk.

"I'll be right back."

The diner music played faintly in the background as I darted back to my locker in the breakroom and returned with my wallet.

"Before I forget, I believe I owe you this," I announced before presenting him with my ID. "Thanks again for giving me time to get my sh—my stuff together. I surrendered my entire day off to the DMV, but I got it."

"Thanks. I'll scan it and get it right back to you."

"Sounds good."

"For what it's worth, I'm glad I didn't have to let you go. Somethin' about having you around lights up the place."

I smiled politely. "Thanks... Hey, uh, does the offer still stand?"

"What offer is that?"

"You showing me around the city."

"Sure. You got anywhere special you wanna go?"

"You tell me, mister tour guide."

"Well, how about we start at Edgewater Falls? You'll get to see it up close, and who knows, maybe it'll clear your head, too."

I tilted my head in a yes. "Sure... when?"

"How about tomorrow morning around eight?"

"And just so we're clear, this isn't like a date or anything, right? Since you are technically my boss. I don't want anyone getting the wrong idea," I stated.

Don shook his head while jerking his shoulders in a careless shrug. "Nah. Nobody goes on dates at eight o'clock in the morning."

"So, like a guided tour?" I snickered.

We shared a laugh. "Yeah, exactly."

* * *

DON and I met the following day, at the beginning of the trail at Edgewater Falls, at eight o'clock sharp. He was wearing a hunter-green Nike hoodie and matching joggers with running shoes on his feet, while I had on a windbreaker jacket, leggings, and a belly full of butterflies. His smile ambushed me as soon as our eyes met. I couldn't tell if the chirping of love birds was real or only in my head.

"Good morning," he greeted me.

"Good morning. Uh, here you go," I said, handing him a sealed Ziploc bag of muffins.

"What's this?"

"Homemade chocolate chip muffins, also known as the byproduct of another sleepless night. I like to bake in my spare time, in this case, overbake. So, you're welcome."

"Wow, thanks."

"I heard if you walk while eating them, the calories don't count."

"Yeah? Where you hear that at?"

"It had to be Oprah." I giggled.

A smile ruffled his lips. "Let's see what these homemade muffins talkin' 'bout," he said skeptically before unsealing the bag and taking a bite.

"Well?"

I watched his eyes roll back in his head while he eagerly chewed what he had in his mouth to take another bite. "These are amazing, Neema."

"Yeah?"

"Hell yeah! We might have to sell these at the diner."

My lips danced around a smile. "Stop."

"No. I'm serious, Neema. These are delicious. What's your secret?"

"What makes you think there's a secret?"

"For somethin' that tastes this good and moist, there's always a secret."

"I have to leave some things up to the imagination."

"Hey, let it never be said that I didn't shoot my shot to try and find out the secret formula," he joked. "These are amazing, though. Next time you feel like overbaking, bring them into the diner."

"I'll do that. Thank you."

"No. Thank you. I haven't had anything this good since I was a kid. My mama used to make homemade everything all the time. Everything was from scratch, and eventually, the diner was born."

"I know you said you've been here your whole life, but you never said why you stayed. Can't just be all for the diner, right?"

He shrugged his athletic shoulders as we casually began to walk and talk along the winding dirt path, with leaves scattered every few steps. "I don't know. After my parents died and all my siblings moved away, I felt like it was on me to stay, y'know? It was on me to see it through. Besides, staying here, running the diner, it makes me feel close to them and lets me know I'm doing the right thing by sticking around."

"That's really nice."

"So, uh, are delicious chocolate chip muffins the only thing you like to bake? Or are there other treats on your menu?" he inquired, changing the subject.

"Uh, well, it all depends on what I have on hand at the time. Sometimes, it's brownies or a cake, maybe cookies."

"You ever think about opening your own bakery?"

I quickly shook my head. "Me? Oh, no. I'm good at baking, but it's only a hobby."

"You sure? The world doesn't know what it's missing out on. On second thought, maybe I'll keep your goodies all to myself."

Contentment hooked my lips. "Maybe you should," I replied.

Swooping branches hung overhead as we walked through areas of shade and sunlight. As we continued to walk the curvy trail, I noticed Don would wave at every three or so people we passed. "You must be a super familiar face around here."

"They know me from the diner, that's all. Do you have any friends here in The Falls yet?"

"Just you," I answered as my shoes scraped over the uneven path.

A warm smile spread across his face as the cool, early morning breeze whistled through the branches. "Lucky me."

"Honestly, I'm not into all the social connections and stuff. I've learned that few people are worth the time and effort, but you...you're different. I can tell," I admitted.

"Oh yeah? How so?" he asked, kicking one of the scattered pinecones in his path.

I shrugged my weary shoulders. "I don't know. I guess I'm a true believer in signs."

"What, like soulmates?"

I scoffed. "Soulmates are for people who believe in a merciless creator who watches from afar and finds humor in watching humans mess things up."

His eyebrows perched as he huffed. "Damn, talk about honesty."

"I'm sorry, I didn't mean to offend you; I—"

"Nah, it's cool. I can dig it."

"I guess maybe that's why I move around a lot. You could ask me where I see myself a year from today, and I honestly wouldn't be able to tell you."

"You just go wherever the wind takes you, huh?"

I shot him a nod of agreement. "Exactly."

"Since we're friends, those are your words, not mine. Friends get to know each other, right?"

A chuckle escaped my nostrils. "I guess."

"We can take things nice and easy. I'll start. You already know steak and eggs are my favorite comfort meal. What about you?"

"Definitely Chicago deep dish pizza."

"I've never had authentic Chicago-style pizza, but I guess I can get behind that. So, we covered your favorite comfort food. What's your favorite comfort movie?"

"Comfort movie?" I inquired.

"Yeah. Y'know, like, what's that one go-to movie you'll watch whenever, wherever. The movie you can damn near recite all the lines to. Mine is *New Jack City*."

"Hmm. I think I'd have to say any of the Fridays. Whether it's the first or the third, I know so many of the words, I damn near feel like I wrote the script myself."

He bobbed his head in agreement. "Hell yeah. Those are classic staples in the Black movie hall of fame. It's in the Holy Hood Bible and everything."

I flicked both brows up with laughter. "The Holy Hood Bible?"

"Yeah. I think it's somewhere between the chapter of Uncle Luke and Lil' Jon. Let's fight about it," he stated before unleashing a laugh.

Laughter welled up inside me as we paused at the signpost near the best observation spot overlooking the falls. A few scattered tourists were posing for pictures, and Don even offered to snap a few. I stood in a trance, silently taking in the breathtaking views of the waterfall as the spraying water smashed into the slippery rocks.

Don took his place beside me and twisted his neck in my direction. "Yo, I wanna ask you somethin', but I don't wanna make it seem like I'm trying to be all in your business," he said over the roar of the water.

I drew in a deep breath as my heart drummed against my ribs. The air smelled like wildflowers and wet stones. *Please don't ask me about my ID. Please don't ask me about my ID.*

"What is it?"

"What do you dream about?"

I eased out a breath through my nostrils, thankful he hadn't questioned the legitimacy of my ID. "Scary shit."

"Like what? C'mon, I'm not scared of things that go bump in the night. You can tell me."

I gazed at his smooth skin before looking into his bright, brown eyes. "I don't know. I guess it just depends. Sometimes they are new bad dreams, and sometimes they are recurring."

"What happens in the recurring dream?"

I shook my head, knowing I couldn't discuss it with him. We were still strangers in my eyes. My throat rattled before I spoke, ready to change gears a bit. "I don't have a problem falling asleep. The issue is staying asleep or staying in one place these days."

"What do you mean?"

I paused, momentarily halting under the wide-open sky to hear the wind feathering through the water. "I've kind of been... sleepwalking a little."

"Sleepwalking? Like for real sleepwalking?"

"I don't know of a fake kind of sleepwalking."

"Damn. For how long?"

"Just a few weeks now."

"A few weeks? Have you ever talked to anyone about it or seen someone?"

"No."

"So what have you done about them?"

"Nothing. Even the slightest noise will take me out of a dead sleep, and sometimes I'll wake up in random places in my apartment and don't remember how I got there. It's scary."

He gave a clipped nod. "Sounds like it."

"Hope I haven't freaked you out."

"It'll take a lot more than a few bad dreams to scare me away."

I smiled at the idea of him sticking around. "Good to know."

* * *

THE AIR WAS thick with the tang of sweat and lemony-scented antibacterial cleaner as soon as I walked through the gym doors later that evening. I walked past the mirror panels along the wall, the pro shop selling whatever nutritional supplements were trending, and pulled a couple of antibacterial wipes from the bucket. I wiped down the machine before hopping on the empty treadmill. My feet relentlessly pounded the mat, running as fast as I could as if trying to outrun my shadow. The timer beeped, and the machine automatically slowed down. My fatigued muscles quivered, feeling the pleasant burn of my warmup.

Sweat slid down my spine as I glanced at my phone to check the time. I had ten minutes until the yoga class I'd shown up for would start. After a few repeat nights of not sleeping and one desperate Google search later, I figured I'd try yoga to help me relax and hopefully sleep better. After wiping down my equipment, I took a swig of water from my bottle, silently rejoicing in its coolness. I found the room with the scheduled group yoga class and walked inside.

"Excuse me. Is this the beginner yoga class?" I inquired to the first woman I saw.

She had tawny brown skin and wore a matching sky-blue sports bra and leggings set. Her raven black hair was pulled into a high ponytail with a gray headband around her edges. A gold hoop sat in her right nostril, and a thin gold chain laid around her neck. "Hi. Yes. You're in the right place."

I sighed, relieved. "Great. Thanks."

"Do you have a mat?"

"Oh, um—"

She shook her head. "It's fine. I always bring a couple extra. Grab one from the corner over there."

"Thank you so much."

She smiled before tipping her body forward. "*Namaste.* Enjoy the class."

A few minutes later, the same woman stepped up to the front of the class, rolled out her mat, and planted her feet on it before introducing herself.

"Welcome. *Namaste.* I'm Mel, your yoga instructor this evening. You're all here today for various reasons, but you probably have one thing in common: seeking peace. My job is to help guide you on your journey to find what you seek. I do this by teaching you how to get your mind and body on one harmonious accord, through various poses and breathing techniques. There's no need to be nervous. I'm not looking for perfection today, only effort. Let's get started."

The class ended forty-five minutes later, and I headed into the locker room to retrieve my things before heading to the bus stop. Just as I swung my bag over my shoulder and slammed the locker door, I met up with Mel, walking out of the locker room simultaneously.

"Hey, I've seen you here a couple of times, right?" she inquired.

"Yeah."

"I'm Mel, short for Melanie."

"Neema," I responded. "I didn't know you were an instructor."

She shrugged her toned brown shoulders. "Only a few times a week. Did you enjoy today's class?"

"Mmhm. I'm still new to this yoga thing, but I'm sure you knew that from taking one look at my wobbling poses."

She chuckled. "We all have to start somewhere."

"Yeah."

"So you're new to yoga?" she asked, sipping from her rhinestone-covered water bottle.

"Yeah. I read somewhere that yoga helps with anxiety and sleep, so here I am."

"What exactly are your pain points?"

"Just the sleep... or lack thereof."

"Well, yoga can help improve your sleep, but it sounds like you may be interested in Yoga Nidra," she suggested.

"That's something different than what we did today?"

A soft laugh escaped her full lips. "Yeah. You said you have trouble with sleep, right?"

"Yeah."

"Well, that form of yoga helps you rest."

"Really?"

"Yeah. If you start to practice it regularly, it can help calm your mind. I don't know about you, but my brain always has a million tabs open."

"My thoughts are always bouncing from one thing to another," I resonated.

"It can also help reduce anxiety."

"This seems to be checking all my boxes."

"You have to discover what is right for you."

"No way to know until I try, right?" I asked, bobbing my left shoulder with a shrug.

"Exactly. I can tell you more if you're interested."

I bobbed my head. "I think I am."

"Cool. Let's meet up for coffee tomorrow, say, around eleven?"

"I'm working tomorrow. Can we aim for the day after?"

"Sure. What time?"

"Eleven works."

"Cool. Put your number in my phone, and I'll send you the address to the little café called Teatime and Tulips that I like downtown. They've got a cool underground bookstore in the back. It's a vibe."

A smile lifted the corners of my lips. "Sounds good. Thanks," I said, tapping my digits into her phone.

Four

DON

THE FOLLOWING WEEK ROLLED AROUND, and I found myself staring at the large clock on the far wall, shaped like a black cat. The tail swung from side to side as I watched the long hand reach the five while the shorthand was settled onto the number twelve. The bells on the door jingled against the glass as the lunch crowd started to pour in.

I hadn't been alone with Neema since our "guided tour," but she seemed to enjoy the close-up view of the falls. As much as I enjoyed being in her presence, I was her boss and couldn't let her know she was the main attraction in my four a.m. thoughts, no matter how badly I wanted to.

I pushed my jumbled thoughts of her aside and grabbed my things before leaving the back office. My feet shuffled toward the door as I smiled politely and nodded in recognition at my regular patrons. I caught a glimpse of Neema refilling a cup of steaming coffee for a customer in a nearby booth, and I decided to approach her.

"Hey, you know I was serious about selling your muffins here in the diner, right?"

"Now I do."

I shot her a quick smile. "Good. I've got somewhere to be, but I'll see you later, and we can hash out the details," I said before tipping my chin and exiting the diner.

After putting fresh lilies on my mother's grave for her birthday in a few days, I headed to the bank for a meeting with the loan officer. My shoulder pushed against the heavy glass door before I journeyed through the S-shaped maze of ropes until I stood before a female teller.

"Good afternoon, sir. How can I help you?"

"Hi. I have an appointment with Jason Wilson at one o'clock."

"Sure. Have a seat in the waiting area over there, and I'll let Mr. Wilson know you've arrived," she informed me, pointing to four chairs to her left.

"Sure thing." I agreed with a nod.

My eyes ping-ponged from wall to wall, observing the posters about retirement funds and investing in the future. Just as I was about to pull out my cell phone, I heard a male voice call out my name.

"Mr. Saintsbury? Hi. I'm Jason Wilson, one of the loan officers here. Come on back to my office, and let's chat."

* * *

THIRTY MINUTES LATER, I pushed through the thick glass entryway and spilled back into the parking lot with a chip on my shoulder. The loan officer started with big smiles and small talk for the first five minutes before denying me a loan, citing my need for a more significant cash flow, and without another investor onboard to help offset some of the costs, there was nothing he could do. The last thing he said before sending me out the door was to come back and see him if my financial circumstances changed in the next thirty to sixty days. It was the third bank I'd been to and the third denial I'd gotten.

I'd done everything in my power to try and secure a business loan to remodel the diner and give it some serious upgrades, inside and out. It took big bank to rebrand, which I didn't have. With every no I received, it became harder not to want to give up.

I flopped back into the driver's seat when my phone dinged with a new email. Aggravated with the world, I snatched up the phone with a grimace across my face and unlocked it. I received another email from the interested buyer, upping their final offer price from seven hundred and fifty thousand dollars to a million.

"Holy fuck." I grumbled, immediately calculating the four-way split in my mind, which equaled a quarter of a million for each of my siblings and me.

I saw dollar signs just imagining having that much money at once. With that money added to what I had already saved, I could almost do everything I wanted to upgrade the diner, but to get it, I had to agree to sell the last puzzle piece of my family's legacy. And I wasn't okay with that shit.

* * *

LATER THAT AFTERNOON, I returned to the diner and sat at a booth in the back, crunching numbers. That is, whenever I wasn't sneaking glances at Neema. For the most part, she looked happy, but the look on her face when she thought no one was looking concerned me. It was as if she were trying to outrun her shadow.

"Hey, you," she greeted me.

"What's up?"

"Not much. The last of the lunch crowd just left, so it'll slow down for a few hours until the dinner crowd comes in."

"Well, in that case, sit. Take a load off for a minute and join me," I insisted.

"You sure?"

"Yeah. Besides, we haven't talked since our walk, and I wanted to know if you enjoyed it."

Neema sat across the booth from me and nodded. "I did. Everything was very... green."

"Green?"

"Yeah. All the trees and everything. I don't know. Something about it made me feel one with nature and calm. Plus, green is my favorite color."

"Oh yeah?"

"Yeah. It represents nature, safety, luck, and I can't forget, *money*."

My jaw ticked. Just the mere mention of the word money had me ready to scream. I cleared my throat, trying to bring myself back into the present. "Uh, that's what's up. Any more bad dreams?"

"Only one since," she said with a coy smile.

"Ah, see. We gotta go back then and get you one with nature again to keep 'em away."

Neema chuckled softly. "Yeah. Maybe we should. The falls were beautiful. I can see why people are always tripping over themselves to visit."

I bowed my head a touch before my phone vibrated against the table. I saw my sister Paris's name on the screen and rolled my eyes before quickly pressing decline.

"I hope I'm not overstepping here, but are you... okay?" Neema asked with a concerned expression.

"Me? Yeah. I'm good," I replied with a quick nod.

"Because the look on your face is sayin' you're the one who needs to become one with nature."

"How do I look?"

"Stressed."

I sighed. "I'm just trying to figure out what to do about something."

"Can I help?"

I hoisted a shoulder upward. "I thought you said you were a pretty mediocre listener or something like that."

"I mean, looking around here, it seems like I'm your best option right now, unless you wanna go spill your tea to Anton or Tony in the back."

I chuckled. "Nah. I'm good on that. But uh, there's... this buyer who wants to buy the diner."

Her eyes widened. "Whoa. Buy it and do what with it? Run it themselves?"

"More like tear it down and build a luxury hotel," I informed her.

"Are you serious?"

"Yeah. At first, I ignored it, but now they've upped the offer, and now my siblings are calling me back-to-back, ready to sell at the drop of a dime. I understand the money is good, but damn. Is that all it's about?" I griped.

"It's okay if you don't want to tell me how much."

"Let's just say it went from a lot to a whole lot of money, and it's their final offer, so the pressure is on."

"So what are you going to do?"

"That's the thing. I don't know what to do. One of the hotel reps wants to meet and discuss their vision face-to-face, but I don't know. What would you do if you were me?"

"I honestly think it depends on how much it was and if I thought it was worth it in the long run."

"A million dollars," I mumbled.

"A *million dollars*?" she emphasized quietly. "For a million dollars, I would hear him out for sure."

"That's the thing. I wouldn't be getting a million. It's split four ways between my siblings and I."

"Still, a quarter of a million per person ain't bad. You can do a lot with that type of money."

"I know. What would you buy if it were you?"

"If I had *your* money?" Neema shrugged her stiffened shoulders. "I don't know. I hate taking the bus, so one of the first things I'd probably get would be a car. It wouldn't be too flashy, just something practical that works and can get me from point A to point B with no issues. I might take a two-week trip overseas to explore Europe. I've always wanted to do that." I tilted my head to the side, eyeing her as the corner of my mouth lifted in a smile. "What?" she asked.

"Nothing. It's... nothing. You really think I should hear him out?"

Her shoulders rose and fell. "One conversation can't hurt, can it?"

"I guess you're right."

"I usually am about these things."

"If I go through with this, you have to agree to come with me."

Her eyebrows jutted toward her hairline while she wagged her head. "What? No. No. No. No."

"Please?"

"No. I don't know the first thing about business. I'd only get in your way."

"All you have to do is help me keep my mind from racing away from me."

"And how exactly do I do that?"

"By just being yourself, Neema."

Five

⁂

INDIGO

I STOOD in the café's long line to the cash register while staring at the wall of coffee bean drawers with dozens of labels identifying their origins and flavors. Amongst them I suspected was the perfect combination for someone's latte or cappuccino, but I still didn't know what I would get. I'd never been one for an overly complicated, fancy-ass coffee order, but something about meeting with a potential new friend made me want to try something new.

I claimed a chair by one of the giant glass windows with an angled view of the street while taking the first sip of my milky latte with whipped cream and a caramel drizzle on top. I was sure I was more in love with how it looked than how it tasted, but I slurped it down anyway to keep myself alert. Mel walked in, and I waved her down. She looked different than she did the first time we met. She'd traded in her secure bun for a silk press, showcasing the bouncing curls in her long mane. After grabbing a coffee, she tossed herself into the chair across from me before posing prettily. She'd gone from bargain-store yoga attire to haute couture. I knew new money when I saw it.

"Sorry I'm late," she said before hanging her designer purse off the back of the chair.

"No problem. Had I known this was a more formal meeting, I would've dressed better," I told her.

"Girl, you look fine. Trust me; this is all for show. If I had it my way, I'd live in my gym clothes twenty-four-seven. I have a couple of appearances this morning with my husband."

"*Appearances*? He sounds famous. What's he do?" I inquired while glancing at the sparkling emerald-cut diamond ring wrapped around her finger.

"Uh, he serves under Mayor McAdams as the city administrator."

"Wow? Like the right hand to the mayor? That's a big deal, right?"

Her shoulders bounced with a shrug. "Depends on who you ask, I guess. A lot of people around here are ready to see some real change, y'know? So he's running against the incumbent in the election this fall, which means the twins are with the nanny, and I'm on the campaign trail dripping in designer."

I tipped my head once. "You're quite the busy bee, huh?"

She nodded avidly. "*Too* damn busy, but enough about me. Let's talk about you. So you're new here?"

"I've been here for a few months now, but still feel like a fish out of water most days."

"No friends?"

I shook my head. "No. Not really," I said as my mind drifted to Don. "Well, maybe there's *one*."

"*One*?" she asked, eyebrow lurching toward her hairline.

I smiled at her in a slightly absent way. "Yeah. We're cool. He's shown me a few places around the city."

"*He*? Mmhm."

"What?" I quizzed.

"I know we just met and all, but I feel a crush brewing if there's not already something going on between you two."

"A what? No. What is this, high school? We're just... friends. We're cool. It's nothing," I assured her.

Mel tossed her hands up. "Yeah, sure. Whatever you say. I'm not trying to be all in your business or anything. I'm sorry if I overstepped."

"It's fine, really."

"You'd think I'd be overly comfortable talking to strangers since I teach classes, but if I'm being honest, I don't have many friends."

"Are you not from here either?"

"I am, but high school was a decade ago, and the friends I had then are more like acquaintances now. Besides, females around here can be... cliquey, especially ones that run in certain circles," she stated in a lowered voice.

I leaned forward. "Certain circles?"

She looked over her shoulder before also leaning in. "You're still new here, so I don't want to paint a certain picture of the city before you've gotten to sink your teeth into it and formed your own opinion, *but...*"

I smirked, totally intrigued. "Of course, there's a *but.*"

"A few months ago, there was this huge, messy ass exposé called *'The 'Baddie Body Snatcher' Baby Daddy Scandal'* that outed a lot of important people in this city's upper crust."

"Some of those *acquaintances* you mentioned?"

"No comment," she said as her eyelashes fluttered toward the café's cathedral ceiling.

"Who in the hell would release something like that?"

"Someone looking for a hell of a lot of trouble, I guess."

"Sounds like it."

"Only when the article was released, the girl who wrote it was dead."

"Dead?"

"Murdered."

"Murdered?" I asked, unable to stop repeating her. "Hold up. Are you fuckin' with me?"

"Wish I was. Apparently, they arrested the guy who did it, which happened to be the guy she outed in the article."

"How'd she out him?"

"For providing his *high-paying* clients with sexual favors for money, one being the police chief's wife."

My brows heightened in surprise. "His wife? Oh yeah, that's first-class messiness right there," I stated before burying my nose in my cup.

"Trust me, the Potomac Falls tea is *always* piping hot."

"Always?"

"*Always,*" she reiterated before shaking her head. "I'm sorry I've gotten us completely off track from what we were supposed to be meeting about today."

"I will gladly continue listening to you spill the tea. That's a lot more interesting than my insomnia."

"How'd you sleep last night?"

"Eh, so, so," I responded before reaching inside my bag to pull out a plastic tub with a teal lid. "That reminds me... I brought you these."

I placed the tub between us on the table. "What is it?"

"Homemade blueberry muffins. Apparently, when I don't sleep, I bake. Since we were meeting at a café, I figured I'd save us a few bucks by bringing our own bites."

Mel smiled wide and brightly before pulling out a muffin from the container. "What a beautiful and thoughtful idea, Neema. Thank you."

"You're welcome. So take a bite and tell me all about Yoga Nidra. I wanna know everything."

* * *

DAY TURNED into night as I entered the upscale hotel lobby, searching for the restaurant inside. My heels click-clacked against the marble tile as I sailed through the large open area, wearing a knee-length black dress that hugged my curves in all the right places. My short haircut was slicked down on the sides with a few longer pieces from the top swooped over my right eyebrow. I passed tall vases filled with over-sized silk flower arrangements and marveled at the giant water wall before seeing Don standing by the restaurant's entrance with his phone glued to his ear. He looked to be in a deep conversation for a few seconds before ending the call. The flustered look on his face melted away when he saw me and walked over.

A smile jotted across his lips. "Hey. I'm glad you could make it. You look... amazing," he said, eyeing me from head to toe.

My lips danced around a smile. "Thanks. You look nice yourself," I replied, observing the crisp black button-up shirt that clung to his biceps and the tailored black slacks and dress shoes he wore.

"You nervous?" I asked.

"It's that obvious, huh?"

"Don't be."

Don cast his eyes down to the watch adorning his left wrist. "It's almost time to get in there. How do I look?"

I giggled. "Like a million bucks, no pun intended."

A soft chuckle escaped his lips, and I saw his entire body relax. To my surprise, he grabbed my hand, laced his fingers in mine, and escorted us to the hostess area to get our table. A young hostess with streaks of hot pink in her hair guided us through a maze of crowded tables and booths before stopping at a table where a white man was already seated.

He looked at us with a half-cocked smile before standing, buttoning his suit jacket, and reaching for Don's hand. "Mr. Saintsbury, hello. I'm Gavin Winters. Thank you for allowing me to speak with you this evening."

Don reached out to shake his hand. "No problem. This is my date, Neema Ellison. I hope you don't mind that she will join us tonight."

"Of course not. The more, the merrier! Please, both of you, have a seat."

We sat beside each other on the opposite side of the table from the man who looked to be in his mid-to-late thirties. I fixed my eyes on the sweating glass of ice water on the square napkin while listening to Gavin and Don jump straight into business. Gavin pulled out a thin binder with page protectors and started flipping through it.

"I'll be sure not to waste too much of your time this evening and jump right into things. The hotel we're currently dining in is one of four brands under the Waterson Group hotel portfolio. I wanted us to meet in this hotel so that you could get a feel for what you and the people in this city would be experiencing when they stayed. Each hotel under our portfolio has its own luxurious feel to it. Each room has high thread count sheets and soft, hypoallergenic, down feather pillows to ensure an incredible sleeping experience. We've got five-star quality food for breakfast, lunch, and dinner. We've got an Olympic-sized pool and state-of-the-art gym equipment. There's something for everyone to fall in love with. So? What do you think so far? Any questions or thoughts before I move into some demographic data?"

I sat with my lips clamped tight, unable to understand why it seemed like Gavin was trying to sell Don on buying the hotel when the hotel group wanted to buy what Don owned.

Don cleared his throat before speaking. "It all sounds nice... but frankly, I don't think what you're looking to do is more important to this city than my family's diner."

"Excuse me?" he asked, his head cocked to the side.

"Listen, I'm sure you've done all your market research on the location, the population, and all those other things. And while reading a few online reviews or skimming over our website is cool, you have no idea my establishment's impact on the people of this city.

"*A Taste of Heaven* isn't just some local family diner. It's a black-owned business that's been providing comfort through food for this community since 1985. It has *never* been sold, only passed down from my parents to my siblings and me. Around here, our diner is known for our exceptional service, at-home atmosphere, and affordable, homestyle meals. You'll get good food, conversation, and an all-around good time when you come through our doors. Our crab cake and eggs breakfast has been a staple on the menu since our doors first opened, and it's been attracting people from up and down the interstate for almost forty years."

Gavin raised his hand to stop Don's soapbox speech so that he could get a word in. "Trust me, Mr. Saintsbury, I understand the backstory and the personal ties you have to this diner and the area, but I want to make sure you understand the bigger picture here. Building a new Waterson Group hotel in the city is a good thing. It will bring more to this community than good food and conversation. It will bring new jobs for the residents and tourists, which means more revenue."

I could feel Don's leg bouncing anxiously underneath the table. "I promise, taking away *A Taste of Heaven* means taking the soul out of the city."

"I don't mean to interrupt, but I have a question," I said.

Don and Gavin turned to me, and I cleared my throat. "Have you been inside the diner before, Mr. Winters? Or tried the food?"

He shook his head. "I haven't. I just flew into town earlier today."

"And when do you leave?"

"Um, I believe my flight leaves around one-thirty tomorrow afternoon."

"Then I think before you return to your big corporate office, you should take a minute to see what you'd be robbing the community of if this deal goes through. Everybody's gotta eat, right?"

He tipped his head forward. "Yeah. You're right about that."

We got up to leave, and I followed a few paces behind Don, sure to give him the space we both knew he needed, but he refused to ask. We spilled out onto the small city street, silently walking past the post office, coffee shop, nail salon, and ice cream parlor before he spoke up.

"Thanks for what you did back there."

"No problem. I have to say I was pretty impressed with how you schooled him back there. I didn't know the diner had such a rich history in the city."

"Yeah. That's why I'm fighting so hard to keep it."

"I know this isn't my business, but why are you the only one fighting when it seems your siblings are hard-pressed to sell?"

"Because my sisters look at this place like a burden or a dark reminder."

"And your brother?"

Don's shoulders rose and fell. "Your guess is about as good as mine on that one. We haven't spoken in years, so it's no surprise he's the only one I haven't heard from about this shit."

"Is that a good thing, or…"

"Good for now. He's the one keeping things divided. Whenever he decides to crawl out from whatever rock he's under, I'm sure my sisters will be on his ass about selling, too. If he turns on me and wants to sign, it's a wrap. I'm not sure I can hold out forever."

"I'm sure you'll make the right decision."

"What makes you so sure?"

"I don't know… Call it women's intuition."

"Ah, can't argue with that."

My eyes caught the colorful flower basket hooked onto the light post a few feet ahead before I stopped in my tracks. I couldn't stop Mel's words from earlier swirling around in my head about a crush, and I wondered if I was the only one with feelings. "Hey, uh, can we rewind to the part where you said I was your date? I thought we—"

Don cut me off. "I know! I'm sorry. It just sort of slipped out, and then when it did, I just went with it. I hope I didn't make you feel uncomfortable," he replied.

"No. It's not that... I don't know. It's fine," I said, wagging my head from side to side.

"Are you sure?"

I trained my glance down at the cracks in the sidewalk before drawing my eyes back up to his. "Yeah. I'm sure," I answered before glancing over his shoulder. I noticed the door was propped open to a shop with a neon sign titled *Readings by Tabitha* in the window. "Have you ever been to a psychic before?"

Don shook his head. "Nah. You?"

"No, but who knows? Maybe Tabitha will read your palm and help you decide."

"Or it could be a complete waste of money and time."

"That too."

He looked at the open door and then back at me. "Fuck it, let's do it."

We stepped inside, and the smell of incense tickled my nose as I gazed around the small area. There were strings of lights hung around the ceiling and a few burning candles on top of a glassed-in case with a sign-in book on top. After signing in, an older foreign woman stepped through the beaded divider between the waiting area and private rooms in the back reserved for psychic readings. She wore oversized hoop earrings and a beaded turban on her head.

"How can I help you?"

I spoke up first. "He'd like to get a reading."

"*We* would like to get readings," Don interjected. "Are you Tabitha?"

"I am. How did you hear about me?"

"We're just two thrill seekers who walked in off the street," he answered her.

"There are three different readings we do here. Tarot readings are twenty-five dollars, tea readings are fifteen dollars, and palm readings start at ten dollars per hand, depending on how in-depth your reading is. There are no refunds."

"I think I'm going to try a tea reading," Don told her.

I didn't know what it was about being in a place like that, but it suddenly awakened a sense of curiosity in me. "I'll do a tarot reading," I answered.

"Paying together or separately?"

"Together is fine," Don answered.

"That will be forty dollars," she informed him.

After he paid, another older woman with a foreign accent joined her before taking Don to the back.

"Good luck," he teased.

"Yeah. You too."

"Come with me, ma'am." Tabitha waved as I followed her through the beaded curtain.

I tipped my chin forward before catching a fleeting glimpse of a Siamese cat wandering the back of the shop. We entered a private room where Virgin Mary and Baby Jesus figurines with rosaries draped over them sat on the table. Dark purple curtains were draped around the walls as eerie music played in the background.

"Have a seat, and we will get started shortly," she insisted.

I'd never had an actual psychic reading before, but I was a skeptic through and through. I knew I wasn't going to talk about anything specific. I sat in the cushioned chair across from her, unsure why my palms were sweaty.

Tabitha placed her folded hands on top of the table. "Before we begin, I want you to know that if I see bad news for you, I will not tell you."

I cocked my head to the side. "Why not?"

"I am only in the business of delivering good news. Are you ready to begin your reading?"

"Um, sure."

I watched her cut the deck and shuffle the tarot cards before me. "I want you to close your eyes, draw a deep breath, and try to clear your mind. Now, focus on what you are seeking clarity on."

"What do you mean?"

"Such as life, love, or maybe your career. The cards may bring you the answers you seek and some you don't."

"Okay."

"Draw four cards with your left hand."

"Why my left?" I inquired, questioning everything.

"It is closer to your heart."

I followed her instructions and drew the cards one by one, and she studied them quietly. "The cards reflect everything about your life—your past, present, and future."

"What do you see?"

"The Seven of Swords is in the upright position, which means deception and trickery. Next, you drew the Six of Swords, which was also upright. That represents moving and transition. You're new to the area?"

"Yes," I answered.

She continued. "The next card you drew was the upright Five of Swords. This card represents your uninhibited ambition and your win-at-all-costs mindset. Is anything I'm saying resonating with you?"

My hands trembled as I stared at the tarot cards on the table. "I don't know... maybe some of it."

"The final card you drew was the reversed Four of Swords, which means restlessness. You have trouble sleeping, don't you? And sometimes... you walk in your sleep. You are afraid of something... of someone from your past," she stated as more fact than a question.

My face turned ashen as the hair lifted on my arms. I swallowed hard, unable to speak. Tabitha reached out to touch my hand and stopped mid-reading before lowering her head.

"What? What's wrong?" I asked, finally able to string words together.

She asked me, "Who is this mahogany-eyed man I see coming to your door who holds a lot of feelings for you?"

My eyebrows drew together as shivers nipped my spine. "I'm sorry, but I think I've had enough," I confessed before quickly pushing away from the table and scurrying out of the shop.

The faster I tried to distance myself from the shop, the harder it became to move. I felt like I was treading through the water until I found a seat on a bench a few feet away. I was utterly unnerved as my lashes blinked back tears. The more I tried to put the reading out of my mind, the more it seemed to cement into my brain.

"Fuck," I mumbled, still trying to shake it off.

Moments later, Don came out of the shop, looking around for me. I gave him a quick wave before he joined me on the bench. "What are you doing all the way out here?"

"Needed some air," I answered.

"How'd your reading go?"

"It was... okay, I guess. Yours?"

Don's shoulders rose and fell. "I can't lie. That shit kinda fucked me up back there."

"What happened?"

"I drank from the teacup and swirled the tea leaves around before she looked at them."

"Did she see anything interesting or at least helpful?"

"From the jump, she told me a great accomplishment was in store for me."

"That's good, right? Anything else insightful?"

"She asked if I got headaches sometimes and could pinpoint where they cluster on the left side of my head, which was trippy. Other than that, I was ready to brush it off, but I couldn't shake this feeling I had."

"What feeling?"

"I don't know, like I was still hungry for more insight, and then out of nowhere, she said the wildest thing. She said that I was torn over something and needed to decide. Then she said to focus on the outcome I wanted, not the outcome I was afraid of."

"That's insightful."

"My mother would say something similar. Growing up, she would always repeat this quote: Everything you want is waiting on the other side of your fear. I don't know. It resonated with me like I could still feel her with me after all this time."

"That's beautiful. I'm glad you got to experience that."

"Her birthday just passed not too long ago."

"What was her name?"

"Angela."

"That's a pretty name."

"Yeah. She was beautiful, and I'm not just saying that because she was my mama. It was like she always knew the right thing to say at the right time."

"That's what great mothers are supposed to do, right?"

"Yeah. I guess so, but I don't know. It's been ten years, and I miss her like it happened yesterday. I miss her and Pops both."

"I'm not sure if that feeling ever goes away, unfortunately."

"You talk like you know from experience."

"I know loss, and I know grief, too. The three of us go way back."

He chuckled. "Old sandbox friends, huh?"

"Something like that."

"How do you power through?" he inquired before stationing his eyes on mine and leaning in.

His face was so close to mine that I could smell the woodsy, masculine scent of his cologne. I watched his gaze drop to my lips as I tried to figure out what to say. Before I could respond, his arms enveloped my waist. His touch sent a glitch to my heart. Suddenly, all my loud thoughts and bone-chilling fears blurred before disappearing. In its place was desire, which was something I hadn't allowed myself to feel in a long time. It was almost as if I was having an out of body experience, watching my body act on its own accord, betraying everything my brain knew to be true.

My heart hiccupped with excitement as I smoothed my hand down the back of my hair, stopping at the nape of my neck. "I-I—"

Without warning or permission, he pressed his warm lips against mine. It was soft at first... gentle. His hand locked around the back of my neck, holding my lips against his for as long as I'd allow. I gripped the bench's armrest, unsure if I wanted to push him away or allow him to slip his tongue inside my mouth. Then, out of nowhere, my eyes drifted closed, and I leaned in deeper. My fingertips clung to his muscles as I threw all caution to the wind. I gently grazed my hands against the rough stubble on his jaw as his tongue danced and swirled around my mouth.

"I'm sorry, but I've wanted to do that all night," he said after gently breaking the kiss.

My lids blinked open and formed a cheeky smile. "Don't apologize. I'm glad you did."

"Well, in that case..."

And for a long moment, we sat frozen in time, making out like a couple of teenagers with no place else in the world to go.

Six

DON

I WAS in the back office, seated behind my desk, when there was a light tap on the door. I saw Neema standing in the gap, waiting to be acknowledged before she entered.

I waved her inside. "Come in."

"Hey. I didn't mean to interrupt, but a woman is asking for you out there."

"Asking for me? Who is she, and what does she want?"

Neema's narrow shoulders shrugged. "She wouldn't give me a name. All she said was you'll know when you see her," she answered before pressing her lips into a fine line.

My eyes rolled toward the ceiling. The last thing I was in the mood for was someone playing games with me or my time. "Aight. I'll be out there in a minute." After a few lingering seconds of her standing there with her lips pursed while different thoughts swam through her head, I spoke up again. "Is there anything else?"

Her eyebrows jogged up her forehead before she shook her head. "Oh! Um, no, nothing else. I'll let her know you'll be out soon," she replied before hurrying away.

I could tell by her mannerisms that she was curious about who the mystery woman was and my ties to her. After the kiss we shared, we agreed that it was best to take things slow and that we would remain as professional as possible around the diner.

The smell of meat grilling on the fryer wafted past my nose as my legs propelled me out of the back office and across the checkered tile floor to see my oldest sister, Paris. She was nestled in the black leather booth against the far wall. My chest seized up. Like the rest of my estranged siblings, Paris and I hadn't shared the same breathing space in many years, so I knew her dropping in from out of the blue wasn't good. I took a deep breath and sighed before approaching her and announcing myself.

"Paris."

She turned her neck in the direction of my voice. Her hair was twisted into faux locs in a bun on top of her head, with a colorful turban covering her edges. She was seated behind the table, but I could tell she was skinnier than I remembered. Although her smile was bright, bags sat beneath her honey-brown eyes, alerting me to how tired and grayed out her once vibrant tawny-brown skin looked.

"Well, aren't you a sight for sore eyes?" she teased.

"What the hell are you doing here?"

"How long has it been?" she inquired, ignoring my question.

"Too long. So, we can cut the small talk, and you can get to why you're here."

"Let's not act like there's not a million-dollar offer on the table, baby brother. Please, sit."

I eyed her closely when sliding into the booth across from her. "Listen, before you start—"

"No, you are the one who needs to listen because I came here to talk. I spoke to Destiny, and I understand that you want to hold onto this place for sentimental reasons, but we both agree it's time to sell," she said, running her hands over the scratched tabletop with chips around the edges.

"That's your problem. You look at this place and see nothing but old memories that you and everybody else seemed to bury after Mom and Dad died, but you forget I've got those same memories. And unlike y'all, I don't want them to fade. They're all I have left."

"You're the baby, Donny. You didn't get as much time with Mom and Dad as we did, and maybe you—"

I cut her off. "You act like they died when I was seven, Paris. I was almost eighteen when that accident happened."

Instead of responding, she turned her attention to the blinds covering our window and ran her fingertip between the blades before looking at the dust she'd collected on it. "You're right. This place does have a lot of memories. I've tried to bury so many things about this diner and this fucking city, but I can't. It's like it's etched underneath my skin," she mumbled with a grimace across her face.

"Paris, if you would just listen to—"

She cut me off mid-sentence. "Did you know the first time I had sex was back by the dumpster? I was raped by the football team quarterback after homecoming when I was fifteen; real romantic. Oh, and here's another fun fact. I had my first miscarriage in the booth right over there when I was twenty-one," she announced, pointing over my left shoulder.

I lowered my head. "Please, stop, aight? I'm sorry, Paris. I never knew you went through all of that."

"How could you? You were the baby, Donovan. We shielded you from everything!"

"And then you left me here."

"You were almost nineteen when we left, and you had the same opportunities to leave when we got our shares from Mom and Dad's life insurance policies. It's not my fault you didn't get out when you had the chance."

"Leaving wasn't an option for me. Mom and Dad would've been turning over in their graves if I did that."

She rolled her eyes. "Something tells me they would've been just fine."

"I may be the baby of the family, but I'm the only one who stood ten toes down in this shit when everyone else disappeared. I don't understand why you can't see this place's importance to me and this entire community. I have a lot of ideas on how I want to renovate this place and bring in even *more* business."

She held up her hand to stop me. "Don—"

I shook my head and continued. "Just hear me out before you automatically shoot me down."

Her eyes rolled skyward. "Fine."

My sister's disinterest in what I had to say didn't stop me from telling her anyway. "I want the chance to turn this place around. I've been trying to get an angel investor to come in and help me revamp the place. I'm talkin' new floors, booths, and stools at the counter. I want state-of-the-art cooking equipment in the back, and new plumbing for the bathrooms. I've been working with a graphic designer on a new logo, and I even want to add some new things to the menu."

"How exactly do you plan to bankroll this big, shiny new vision of yours?" she asked condescendingly.

I sighed, knowing money was the true root of the issue. I'd been vying for government funding and any other handout to help make my vision come to life. It seemed all I'd been doing since I took over the diner was jumping through one new hoop after the next.

"I haven't secured a grant or an angel investor yet, but—"

Her nose scrunched up as she spoke. "I'm sorry, but it sounds like you need to give up on this dream."

I squinted my eyes at her. "This isn't just some dream or ego-related issue, Paris. This is my family, *our* family's legacy. Don't you have kids? Doesn't that mean anything to you?"

"It means everything to me. That's why I'm here, fighting for my legacy, Donovan. Mine! Not yours and not our parents! And if I don't get this money now, I may not be here long enough to pass anything down to my kids!"

I grunted through my nostrils. "What? What are you talking about?"

A sigh broke past her lips. "I didn't want to have to come here and tell you like this."

My brows twitched toward each other. "Tell me what?"

"The deal isn't the only reason I'm here, Donovan. I have adult acute lymphoblastic leukemia."

I swiped my hand over my mouth, looking at her while she talked but unable to make eye contact. I carefully weighed my words before asking, "H-how long have you known?"

Paris's honey-brown eyes watered as she spoke. "Almost a year now."

"I don't know what to say... It's like I have so many questions jumbling at the tip of my tongue," I confessed.

"Look, I don't feel like getting into too much detail, but my doctor ran a hell of a lot of tests and found out that it has spread to other parts of my body. I've gone through the standard treatments, chemo, radiation... and now my doctor wants to consider chemo with a stem cell transplant."

"A what?"

"My body isn't producing enough healthy blood cells, so this procedure would allow doctors to put healthy stem cells in my body to replace the ones that aren't working."

"When do you have the procedure?"

"Well, for one, it's not cheap. For two, I need a donor. And as my sibling, my doctor says, there's a one in four chance that your cells will match mine. All you need to do is take a blood test to confirm."

"And if I'm a match?"

"You can donate your bone marrow to me."

"And if I'm not?"

"Then I'm praying I can get in touch with our brother."

"You already talked to Destiny?"

She tilted her head in a yes. "She was the first person I visited, but she wasn't a match."

A breath rushed out in a sigh. "So that's why you're here..."

"I'm thirty-two with a husband and two kids. I have a good job with a steady income. I'm not supposed to have ca—I need... to live, Donny," she said, voice breaking. "I'm not asking you to sign your life over to me. All I'm asking you to do is get a simple blood test. That's it."

I kept my head down while my eyes looked up at her from across the table. Although we were sitting close, I couldn't have felt more divided from her. The news of my sister's cancer diagnosis and her asking me to donate bone marrow had thrown me off my game and made the situation even more complex. Before I could find the words to respond to my sister, Neema approached our booth.

"Hi. I don't mean to interrupt. I just wanted to check in to see if you all needed something to eat or drink."

"Well," she paused to dab her eyes before looking at Neema's nametag, "Neema, you *are* interrupting. We're in the middle of a very spirited family discussion, so if you don't mind?" Paris snapped.

Our eyes linked before I spoke up. "Neema, this is my oldest sister, Paris."

She nodded before turning her faded Chuck Taylors in the opposite direction and allowing her legs to carry her away.

"Did you have to be so rude?" I snapped at Paris.

Her nose wrinkled as her shoulders bobbed carelessly. "I wasn't being rude. I simply let her know she was interrupting an important conversation."

We shared a pained glance before I spoke up. "Look, Paris; I'm sorry this is happening to you, but I—"

She waved her hand in the air to stop me. "Don't give me your answer right now. I want you to sit with it for at least twenty-four hours before you decide anything. All I wanted to do was deliver the news straight to your face, just like I did Destiny."

"So, after me, our brother is the next stop on your list?"

Paris inched out of the booth and stood to her feet before hanging her purse over her shoulder. "*When* I get in touch with him, I'm going to persuade him to get on board with accepting that offer, and when it's three against one, I'm not sure what else you're going to be able to do to save this place. Because if it comes down to saving this place or my life, Donovan, you know which one I'm choosing."

Paris pushed through the exit, and I stormed back to the office, slamming the door in my wake. The power struggle between my siblings and me was real. The mounting pressure and ticking clock on my shoulders were even more real. I rolled my neck and shoulders before pulling out my phone. I scrolled through my contacts before landing on my brother's name. The call went straight to voicemail without ringing.

"You've reached Enzo Reid. I can't get to the phone right now. Leave a message at the beep."

"Man, fuck!" I groaned, knocking papers off my desk in frustration. I waited for the beep and then spoke my peace into the receiver. "Hey. It's me, Don. I know it's been a minute... well, more than a minute, but we need to talk about the diner, Zo. It's important, so call me back when you can."

Seven

INDIGO

I SIPPED my protein smoothie in the gym's smoothie shop while drowning out the repetitive clanking of barbells bouncing against the floor with my workout playlist. My shoulders bounced to the beat when someone lightly tapped me from behind. I snatched my earbuds from my ear while flipping around to see Mel waving at me.

Her lips smiled faintly. "I didn't scare you, did I?"

I shook my head. "No."

"I called your name a couple of times before I realized you couldn't hear me."

"Sorry. I was just killing some time before our meeting."

"No problem."

"Thanks for agreeing to meet with me this morning. I'm working the late shift at the diner tonight."

"Diner? Where do you work?" Mel inquired.

"Oh, uh, *A Taste of Heaven Diner*, right off—"

"The bridge. Yeah, I'm familiar," she answered.

"Yeah? I've never seen you come in there before."

"It's been many years since I've eaten there, but from what I can recall, it's good. How's it been, y'know, working there?"

I chuckled. "It's fine. No one has dined and dashed on me yet, if that's what you mean."

We laughed in unison. "Well, that's always a good thing. Who runs that place now?"

"Uh, Don, er, Donovan Saintsbury. You know 'em?"

She bobbed her head slowly. "Yeah. We, uh, went to high school together."

"Small world, huh?"

"Sure is. Should we go ahead and get started?"

I ducked my chin. "Lead the way."

"I'm excited about your one-on-one session today, Neema. I really think this will help you."

"I'm willing to try anything, within reason, of course."

"Our minds are strung out on dozens of our half-baked thoughts, fears, and dreams, and many of us carry that stress to bed. So, when it's time to sleep, we can't figure out how to shut off those thoughts."

"How do you do it?" I asked.

"Yoga Nidra helps."

"If this is why you always look so zen, then I'm ready to start."

I followed Mel into a dimly lit, private room where calming music played. Bending at the knees, we lowered onto the two mats rolled out for us.

"*Namaste*, Neema. I want you to lie flat on your back with your palms turned up," Mel instructed before placing a cylinder-shaped pillow underneath my knees and cushioning my head. "Are you comfortable?"

I dipped my chin. "Yes."

"Now, I want you to close your eyes and, for now, focus on my voice. I will speak slowly and intentionally. I will guide you every step of the way."

"Okay," I replied, closing my eyes and allowing my body to melt into the mat.

"Think about what you want out of our session today. Nothing big. I don't want you to think too hard. If a peaceful rest is what you want to accomplish, we can start with that."

"Yes."

"Okay. Now, I want you to get completely comfortable and draw in slow, deep breaths. With each exhale, allow your body to become heavy like an elephant's leg. As you breathe, I want you to think about a place or a time that makes you feel safe or where you remember being your happiest. Take your sweet time allowing that feeling to wash through you."

Our session ended forty minutes later, and I'd never felt more relaxed. My shoulders were slouched, and my eyes were still heavy as I returned to consciousness.

"*Namaste*, Neema. How are you feeling?"

A slow, sluggish smile drug across my face. "I feel... rejuvenated, relaxed."

"Great. Take your time getting up and gathering your thoughts. I'll be waiting just outside the door when you're ready."

I slowly sat up on my elbows before drawing a deep breath and slowly releasing it. My legs propelled me to the door, feeling almost weightless. As promised, Mel stood there with her cell phone glued to her ear. She pressed a button on the screen before sliding the phone back into her bag.

"All set?" she asked with a preoccupied look on her face, telling me her thoughts were elsewhere.

"Yup."

She shook her head, trying to rid her mind of whatever was troubling her thoughts. "Still feeling relaxed?"

"Definitely. Have you ever thought about opening your own yoga studio?"

"I won't lie and say the thought hasn't crossed my mind, but I've got a lot of other irons in the fire right now, and unfortunately, a yoga studio isn't one of them."

"That's a shame. You've got a gift."

"Thanks, but Theo's dreams are the driving force of my day-to-day life right now."

"Theo? Is that your husband's name?"

"Yeah. Theodore Caldwell."

"You said he's running for office, right?"

"Yeah. Mayor. I was just listening to a voicemail from his campaign manager saying he scheduled a panel interview with a few small business owners around the city. So, that'll suck up another unexpected two to four hours of my day today," she said, sounding unenthused.

"I take it all the press appearances and interviews aren't your thing?"

There was a small hop of her shoulders before she responded. "I'm the wife of an emerging politician, so I guess it's just the nature of the job."

"I guess so."

"And don't get me wrong. I admire what Theo is trying to do around here. He wants the city to do more for its small businesses. It's one of the major things he's talking about on his campaign trail, so today's important."

"Yeah?"

"Yeah. He privately got into real estate a few years back and found some success flipping a few foreclosed properties across the bridge in Seven Pines."

"Oh, so he knows a thing or two about permits and loans and how to make the money flow where it needs to, right?"

"Yeah, sure. He's a better brain to pick than mine about all that stuff. Real estate isn't my jam. It's too stressful, and these days, I'm all about things that bring me peace," Mel stated with satisfaction in her tone.

"Hey, I think I might have someone interested in talking to your husband about all that real estate stuff."

"Oh, yeah? Who?"

"I have a friend who's been trying to get some money to renovate his business. He's been running into roadblocks with getting a business loan, grants, or an investor to help fund the project. You think your husband could offer some advice or point him in the right direction?"

"This friend of yours wouldn't happen to be the same friend you mentioned at the café, is it?"

I rolled my eyes while trying to hold back a smile. "What if it is?"

Mel smacked her hands together in satisfaction. "See! I *told* you I felt a crush brewing! I'm never wrong about vibes, Neema, *never*. It's simply one of my many gifts," she boasted with a soft chuckle.

"Yeah, whatever. Do you think your husband could, I don't know, set up a meeting with him and talk?"

"I can do you one better. We're having a dinner party this weekend. You should come. You and your *friend* who's looking for this investment advice."

My neck wagged without hesitation. "No. It's such short notice, and social gatherings aren't my thing."

Mel's manicured nails reached out and palmed my shoulder. "Neema, it's nothing to add two more people to the guest list. And did I say dinner party? Perhaps it's more like a networking event." Her shoulders twitched as a chuckle burst past her lips.

I bumped a shrug. "I don't know."

"It'll be good food, drinks, and conversation. Plus, a little music and even more drinks! C'mon, I promise it'll be fun."

"Maybe some other time," I said in a hopeful tone.

"C'mon, it's one night. A snapshot in time, Neema. What do you have to lose?"

Knowing how important of a connection her husband could be for Don, I sighed and decided to push my feelings aside for a few hours. "Yeah. Sure. Okay. Send me the information, and I'll make sure we're there."

"Yay!" she squealed.

"Do you need me to bring anything? I don't mind picking up a dessert or a bottle of wine or something," I offered.

"Just yourselves. I've hired a catering staff, servers, and everything."

"A catering staff? This sounds fancy. Is there a dress code I should know about?"

Mel shook her head. "Business casual is fine. I'm not having a four-course meal or anything like that. If it were up to me, I'd be fine with serving a cauliflower pizza with some vintage wine. After all, it's the company that counts, right?"

I dipped my chin. "Yeah. I guess so."

Mel pulled out her phone and started tapping away at the screen. "I just sent you the info. I've got to run, but I'll see you next weekend!" She waved.

I waved back before flipping directions and going the opposite way.

I'd only befriended a handful of women in my lifetime, but Mel seemed like she'd found the balance I'd been searching for. What could it hurt to have another friend or *acquaintance,* as she would say, in Potomac Falls?

* * *

IT HAD BEEN a dull afternoon with the gray sky threatening rain. The sun hadn't dared to peek out from behind the heavy clouds all day, and just like it, I had been doing my best to keep as much distance between Don and me as possible. After my rude encounter the day prior with the woman I later found out was his sister, I'd been giving him his space and minding my business. At closing, the moonlit skies split open, and I noticed water dripping from the roof near one of the back booths.

"Great, just great," I mumbled before going into the back to get a mop and a bucket.

Once I mopped up the water and secured the bucket under the drip with a wet floor sign next to it, I pushed my feelings aside long enough to inform Don of the issue with the leaky roof. My knuckles collided with his office door before I paused.

"Come in," he mumbled from the other side.

I drew in a deep breath of air before pushing the door open. Don was standing behind his desk with his back turned to me, and I found myself silently admiring the full length of his physique. He slowly turned around before arching a questioning eyebrow in my direction. "Did you lock up?"

I nodded. "Yeah."

"Thanks. What else did you need?"

"I came to tell you it's raining..."

"And?"

"And... the roof. The roof is leaking." As sadness clouded his features, he ran his hand over the lower half of his face. "I took care of the water and put a bucket under the leak, so it's under control for now."

"Yeah. Thanks."

I rested my eyes on the half-empty glass of dark liquor on his desk before chewing my bottom lip. *Mind your business, girl. Mind your goddamn business.* Instead of listening to my better judgment, I cleared my throat. "Are you... okay?"

His mouth was set in a hard line. "I'm not, but I will be," he replied as his expression hardened. "I'm sorry about Paris. I've learned to ignore her, but she can be... a lot to others."

I shook my head. "There's no need to apologize. You've made it clear your family life is complicated."

"Well, shit just got even more complex."

"How so?"

"She's sick. She has cancer and wants to see if I'm a match to donate bone marrow. I haven't seen her in years, and she blows in here and drops this fuckin' crazy ass bomb on me and gives me twenty-four hours to give her an answer." He scoffed. "Not to mention, she is still pressing me to sell. My head is still spinning, hence the liquor on my desk."

My head tipped forward in a nod. "Mine would be too."

Don slumped into his chair. "I don't know what I should do."

"Well, what do you *want* to do? It's your choice at the end of the day."

He sighed before plonking his head against the headrest. "I know."

"Don't you have other siblings? Has she talked to either of them about it?"

"My sister Destiny isn't a match, and none of us have been able to get in contact with my brother. I'm the only option she has left."

"Then it sounds to me like you already made your decision."

Don jerked his shoulders in a careless shrug before tossing back the rest of the liquor in his glass. "Guess so."

"I hope you don't take this the wrong way, but you're way too stressed. You should come with me to yoga sometime. I'm not an expert or anything, but it's helping. Whatever it is, you need to focus on something that makes *you* happy."

"Stressed isn't the word. I'm stretched too thin between trying to save this place and now my sister's life. Fuck, man!" he roared.

"You need to relieve some of that stress, again, which is why I recommend doing something that makes you happy, whatever it is."

"I don't know what makes me happy right now outside of you," he confessed.

"Well, lucky you, I'm just what the doctor ordered."

I stepped up behind him and started to massage his shoulders gently. I could feel the tight tension in his muscles. I inched my fingertips up and down the back of his neck, slowly kneading my thumb as I went along.

"Damn, that feels good," he mumbled, closing his eyes.

A laughing huff of air escaped my lips. "Y'know, I only came back here to tell you about the leaky roof, right?"

He rendered a sweet laugh from his lips. "Oh, yeah. Come show me."

"Right now?"

"Yeah." Don grabbed my hand, and I followed him out of his office. "Where's it at?"

"Over there in the back," I said, pointing with my free hand.

We walked over to the tabletop with the green bucket on top of it and looked up at the leaky ceiling. "Hopefully, it'll stop raining soon. I'll see if I can get someone to come out and look at it tomorrow," Don announced with a sigh. He placed himself on the booth's edge, still paying undivided attention to the leak above us. "What's that saying? When it rains, it pours."

I stepped closer to him. "Not to bring it up again, but I'm sorry to hear about your sister."

To my surprise, Don placed his hands around my waist and rubbed the arc of my hip bones with his thumbs. "Thank you."

"For what?"

"Just being you," he replied, eyes lingering on mine.

I looked away, careful not to let him see how nervous I was, as my arms remained at my sides. "Don't look at me like that."

He blew a laugh from his nose with a smirk. "Like what?"

"You know, like what."

"Why not?"

"Because it makes me feel things."

A smile tugged at his lips before he inquired, "Where?"

I paused, first gazing at the bucket, then letting my gaze drift over to his face. "All over."

Don pulled me closer, and I straddled his open lap, allowing his growing erection to cushion against my inner thigh. "You make me feel things too, y'know?" he asked, bringing his lips within the same breathing area as mine.

"Like what?" I inquired, voice hushed against his lips.

The fire of passion burned in the pit of my stomach as I circled Don's neck with my arms. His eyes bore into my soul, a look of desire dancing between us as he held me close. I slowly rotated my hips, beckoning him like a siren's song while grinding my wet panties against his arousal.

"See what you did?"

My eyes retraced their path to his bulge. "Maybe I meant to do it."

Our lips fused and held, speaking of everything we'd left unsaid. The aching tension between us continued to build, threatening to erupt at any given moment. The caress of his tongue against my lips made me dizzy with desire. I reached down, circling his thickness with my hand, and his breath quickened.

Don pulled his lips away from mine. "I know we agreed to take things slow, but if given the opportunity, I would fuck the shit out of you, *respectfully*."

The gentle yet demanding persuasion of his lips against my skin had all my inhibitions going up in smoke. "Fuck taking things slow. I wanna feel you inside me."

When he received the green light, he stood and laid me on the table-top. Don bunched my dress up to my thighs before tossing my legs in the air and sliding my panties completely off.

"They are so wet," he commented.

I smirked, curling up one side of my lips. "See what you did?"

Don licked his lips, and a charge of excitement surged through me as he buried his face between my sweet heat. My back arched to the heavens as his tongue teased the tiny, throbbing bud between my thighs.

"Ooooh my Gooood." I purred beneath his touch.

He slid one of his long, brown fingers inside me while I relentlessly moved my hips against his lips. Moments later, my limbs went boneless as I reeled in wicked delight from an all-consuming climax.

He swiftly dealt with my clothes and his before pulling me to the table's edge and fusing his body against mine. Don entered me slowly, the rhythm of his hips catching mine almost instantly. It was as if our bodies had been made for one another. I caressed his rigid arm muscles as my knees clamped his naked, brown hips.

"You feel so good." He hummed against my lips.

I panted. Don being inside me felt so good. It was tampering with my sanity. "Yes! Yes! It feels so good."

Our bodies remained gelled together as one, and my eyes slid shut in ecstasy as his fingertips grazed my nipples. He continued to drive his hips forward, determined to knock the bottom out of my pussy. But I didn't mind. The way he was throwing the dick made me want to tattoo his initials all over my body.

"Look at me, Neema. Look at me while you take this dick." I flashed my eyes up at him before looking down, watching his caramel-colored abs flex with each dip into my sea of pleasure.

Don carried me over to the counter with my legs still intertwined around his waist. After placing my feet on the ground, he bent me over the counter, and I complied without thought. He rested his hand on my lower back as my ass smacked against his muscular thighs.

"Don, it's so deep!" I squealed, digging my nails into the counter's edge as he thrust upwards inside me.

"Mmm. I love hearing you say my name. Say it again."

"D-D-Donovan!"

His grip around the indent of my waist tightened. "Shit. Throw that wet ass pussy back."

I immediately matched his rhythm and threw it back, begging him not to stop. "Don't stop! Don't stop!"

We took it to the floor behind the counter, and I climbed on top. I slowly rotated my hips while gently biting Don's neck and ear. Something about the tangy taste of his sweat-slicked skin and male scent drove me wild.

"You feel so good, Don!"

He grabbed a handful of my ass before smacking it. I pulled his face to my chest and tossed my head back as I bucked my hips harder and faster, feeling myself on the cusp of my climax.

"Oh shit," he groaned.

My back arched forward, and my toes curled as another shock wave of pleasure rippled through me. I wilted against his panting chest, feeling more satisfied than I had in years. A man like Don was rare. He was a gem that one would need to experience firsthand to believe. Never in my lifetime did I think I'd stumble upon the dangerous mixture of perfection such as him when I set my sights on Potomac Falls. But the closer we got, the more afraid I became that he would find out my secret and what drove me to the city in the first place.

Eight

DON

AFTER MY FIRST taste of her, I had Neema's legs wrapped around my waist every chance I could get. She had quickly become a constant in my life. Being around her became almost as necessary as breathing. Whenever I wasn't inundated with the diner, I spent my free time showing her all my city had to offer. No sooner than the thought of her ran through my mind, Neema popped around the corner of my office door with a smile stretched across her face. "Got a sec?"

"For you, always. What's up?"

"How much do you need to fund your renovation project for this place?"

"Why?"

"Just answer the question," she urged.

"I've saved over a hundred grand, but I need close to half a million. I talked to a couple of contractors around here, and the best quote I got was about two-hundred dollars per square foot."

"I may have potentially found you an angel investor," Neema blurted out.

My brows launched upward. "A what? Neema, I never asked you to—"

"I know! But even if he doesn't personally invest, maybe he can point you in the direction of somebody who can."

"*He*? Who is he?"

"I've been hanging out with a new friend I met at the gym here and there, and her husband may just be the miracle you've been looking for."

"How so?"

"All I know is he's into politics and wants to help small businesses around the area. One meeting won't hurt, right?"

I sighed, knowing I was racing against a ticking timebomb without knowing how much time was left on the clock. "Sure. What's his information? I'll reach out and see if I can set something up."

"It's already done. You're meeting them tonight when we go to their dinner party."

My brows snapped together. "Hold up. A dinner party?"

"Did I say dinner party? I mean, networking thing. Dress business casual and prepare to wow him."

"It would be great if I knew who I was preparing to wow."

"It doesn't matter; just be yourself and explain your vision. You already know all the answers."

* * *

WITH NEEMA SETTLED in my passenger seat, I pulled up to the gated entrance of the Edgewater Estates, one of the city's gated communities where the Potomac Fall's upper crust—a collection of wealthy housewives of elected officials, businessmen, and the police chief alike—rested their heads at night.

"Whose house are we going to?"

"A friend."

"A friend who lives in one of the most lavish neighborhoods in Potomac Falls? I thought you said I was your only friend."

"I made a new one."

"A powerful one at that."

"Relax," Neema suggested. "The GPS says we're almost there."

The heavy gates slowly swung open, and we eased inside, passing by dozens of large, manicured lawns. '*The destination is on your left,*' the GPS stated as I turned and parked alongside the other cars lining the driveway.

"You ready?" she asked.

"Yeah. Let's do this."

Neema's heels tapped against the walkway as we approached the front door. The doorbell chimed loudly throughout the house before a dark-complected man answered the door wearing slacks and a tight-fitting black sweater. He had a fresh haircut with a line cut over the left side, a jet-black beard that stretched from one ear to the other, and a set of chocolate-brown eyes I didn't trust. A bulky gold ring sat on his index finger, with another solid gold band two fingers down.

"You must be Neema." He greeted her with a wide-stretched grin, revealing his straight teeth. They were white and bright against his oak-brown skin. "Please, both of you, come in."

"Mr. Caldwell, hi. It's so nice to meet you. Your wife talks about you all the time," Neema said, outstretching her hand to shake his.

I watched him take her hand in his before kissing it. "Please, call me Theo."

"Okay, Theo," Neema replied with a nervous laugh.

"And the pleasure is all mine. If you think she talks about me a lot, you should hear how long she went on about your muffins. She couldn't stop ranting about them, so it was only right to meet the woman behind them."

"Oh, thank you," she said politely before turning to me. "Theo, I'd like you to meet—"

Before Neema could adequately introduce us, I heard a familiar voice call from above us. "Donny?" Mel stated, my high school nick-name breaking from her lips.

We looked up to see Melanie King or Caldwell, I suspected was her new name. My heart quaked, and I felt my stomach sink. The nerves that fluttered in the pit of my stomach instantly turned to nausea. I knew the city wasn't that big, but my ex was the *last* person I expected Neema to befriend. Mel was my high school sweetheart, but our love story lived and died within the halls of Potomac Falls High School. It had been a decade since we'd seen each other, although we lived within the same city limits. Yet, Mel still had the same telling brown eyes, slim frame, and radiant smile she had as if she were still seventeen. Her hand slid against the polished banister as she descended the stairs wearing a simple black cocktail dress and a look of uncertainty on her face.

"Mel?" I mumbled with my heart in my throat.

"You two know each other?" Neema asked on a hush.

"Know each other? Y-yeah. We do. We—"

Mel cut me off. "We went to high school together," she stated before pulling Neema into a quick hug. "Remember, I think I told you that already when you told me you worked at the diner."

"Oh, right. I think I do remember that now."

"Thank you both so much for coming."

Neema dipped her chin. "Thanks for inviting us. You have a beautiful home."

"Yeah. Thanks for the invite," I added begrudgingly.

"Would you like a tour? I'm sure Mel would love to give you one while Donny and I grab a drink and talk," Theo added while placing his hand on my shoulder.

"It's Donovan," I corrected him.

"Excuse me?"

"My name. It's Donovan. Nobody calls me Donny anymore," I answered.

"That's probably my fault. I'm sorry. It just slipped out. I saw you, and my brain reverted to back in the day, but we aren't in high school anymore."

"We damn sure aren't."

"So, uh, about that tour?" Neema interjected, feeling the energy in the room turn sour.

Mel shot out a quick breath. "Yes. Of course. Let's go."

"Now that the women are gone, can I offer you a glass of scotch?" Theo inquired.

"Yeah. Sure. Thank you."

"Great. Let's go to the back patio, and I'll introduce you to everyone."

I followed him from the foyer down the hall, moving slowly as if my legs were wading through water. He stopped short when we were out of earshot and turned to face me. "Listen, I'm sorry about that back there. I was just following my wife's lead with your name."

"It's not a problem."

"Let's step into the kitchen so I can get you that drink," he offered.

"Sounds good."

He bent his steps toward the mini bar in the kitchen and poured me a fresh glass before refilling his own. I stilled, taking a quick swig of the strong drink. Theo ushered a few steps forward to the screened-in patio.

"Gentlemen, this is *Donovan*. Donovan, this is everyone," he introduced me.

"Hi, I'm Hunter Warren," one man introduced himself. He was a pale white man with red hair and emerald-green eyes.

I reached out to shake his hand. "Donovan Saintsbury."

"Saintsbury? Where do I know that name?" a Black man with big nostrils, who looked in his mid-forties, asked.

"*A Taste of Heaven Diner*."

"Ah, that's it! I used to love coming in there before my doctor made me cut back on all the good stuff to lower my cholesterol," he stated. "I didn't know that place was still in business."

"Been around since 1985," I informed him.

"Is that so?" he asked, face tense, and he swiveled the weight of a crystal highball glass in his hand.

Feeling threatened, I instinctively straightened my posture. "Yeah, it is."

His look softened before he outstretched his hand to mine. "Reginald Brown." He introduced himself without blinking.

"Nice to meet you," I said, giving his hand a firm shake.

I tossed down the rest of my glass rather quickly while listening to all the humdrum chatter around me. I made sure to smile and nod every few seconds to look as if I was paying attention, but I didn't give a fuck. The most interesting thing I learned in the mix of conversation was that Mel was married to the mayor's right hand.

"Bathroom?" I inquired, eyeing Theo.

"Down the hall. It's the second door on the left," he instructed.

"Bet."

One foot overtook the other before I flipped the switch, illuminating the powder room. I hovered over the sink, watching the water race down the drain before splashing a few drops on my face. I ran my palms over the cool granite counter to settle my nerves. Surrounded by high-end fixtures and monogrammed hand towels, I swiveled my eyes up to the mini chandelier above me. I couldn't believe I was standing in Mel's lavish ass house. My eyes shot up to the round vanity mirror as I dried my face and drew in a few deep breaths. I ushered a few steps to the door and paused, seeing Melanie standing on the other side.

"H-hey," she breathed out.

"Hey."

"It's been a long time, huh?"

I dipped my chin. "Yeah."

"H-how have you been?"

"I'm good, Mel."

"Great. That's, um, great. Listen, Donny, I-I mean, Donovan. I didn't know that you and Neema were—"

I shook my head while waving my hand to stop her. "It's cool."

"She said a friend was looking for an angel investor, and I—"

"I said, it's cool."

"Okay, well, um, let me or any of the waitstaff know if you need anything."

A scoff escaped my lips before my brain could stop it. "I'll be sure to do that."

"Did I say something wrong?"

My eyes untangled from hers, only to see Neema standing there, eyes anchored on us. "Hey, I gotta go," I told Mel before stalking off in the opposite direction.

When I made it to Neema, she looked at me with a furrowed brow and crinkled nose as if an odor stung her nostrils. "Everything okay?"

"Everything is fine. Why?"

"Nothing. I'm good. Are you?"

"I'm not feeling too well. I think I'm going to head out."

"Head out? You can't just leave, Neema. I drove us, remember? What's wrong?"

"I know. I was going to go outside and call an Uber or something. I don't want my fickle stomach to mess up your chance to network or whatever you were doing with Mel back there."

"Trust me, it's not what you think, and I'm good. Let's go."

"Are you sure?"

"Yeah."

The beginning of the ride was dead silent until I slowed the car to a halt at a red light. I darted my eyes over to Neema, who had her attention focused on whatever was outside her window.

"How is your stomach feeling now?"

"No change," she answered quickly.

I sighed. "Listen, I understand you were trying to help me by introducing me to those people, but I wish you had told me whose house we were going to before we got there."

"Why does it matter?"

"It usually wouldn't, but this time, it does, aight?"

"Are you going to keep me in the dark, or are you planning to tell me what's going on between you and Mel?"

I sighed. "Listen, I don't know what you think you saw back there, but that was nothing. Nothing is going on between us."

"It may be nothing to you, but from the look on her face, it wasn't to her."

"We didn't just go to high school together, Neema. Mel is my ex."

The car fell silent for a few seconds before a simple word fell off her lips. "Oh."

"Yeah."

"Why didn't you say anything?"

"I would have, had I known whose house we were going to or who you'd been hanging around."

"I didn't know I needed your permission to make other friends."

I sucked my teeth. "You don't. There's just... a class system around here."

"There's a class system everywhere you go."

I sucked my teeth. "You don't understand."

"I'm trying to, but you keep shutting me out."

"People like Mel and Theo don't think we're good enough to be around them."

"What makes you think that?"

"It's not what I think, Neema. It's what I know."

"Well, I don't get that vibe from her at all. Yeah, she has money, but she's different from Theo."

"She's not, aight? Now, can we please drop it? I don't want to ruin what's left of the night."

"Yeah, sure. Fine."

* * *

A WEEK AND A HALF LATER.

I'D JUST RECEIVED an email with the results of my blood test, confirming I was a match to donate my blood marrow to Paris, and hopped on the phone to call Neema. The phone rang a few times before she picked up.

"I hope you're calling about anything other than work since today's my day off," she answered, still sounding like she was being held hostage by her sheets.

"Did I wake you?" I asked, glancing at my watch to check the time.

"Kind of. I was laying here letting my mind wander in a million different directions with my eyes closed."

A slight smile spread across my lips. "You've been sleepin' better?"

"I have... thanks to a certain somebody."

"Well, I'm happy to come put you to sleep whenever and wherever you need me to," I assured her.

"That's good to hear," she said, words stretching out as she yawned into the receiver. "So, what's up?"

"I got the results back from the blood test."

"What's it say?"

"I'm a match."

"Wow. H-how do you feel? Have you told your sister yet?"

"No. You were the first one I called."

"Why me?" she asked modestly.

Although I couldn't see her through the phone, I could tell she was smiling. "You know you my girl now, right?"

"What are you, one of those 'I licked it, so it's mine' type of people?"

I cheesed. "Precisely."

"What about the diner? You *technically* are my boss, and I don't want no smoke from the other employees' thinkin' you're giving me extra special treatment or anything."

"Aren't I, though?" I quizzed with my head tilted to the side.

She smacked her lips. "Shut up!"

I cut free a quick laugh. "I'm joking. You're right. We can keep things between us under wraps and professional at work, but when we're not there, you're all mine."

"You can't keep me to yourself forever, y'know?"

"Damn. You've spoiled my master plan."

"Oh, have I now?" she asked, voice light and airy.

"Hell yeah, girl. I know a good thing when I see one."

"You don't even really know me."

"I know enough to know that I like what I see, and ain't nothin' about to change that."

"Listen, I'm about to take a shower. Call me back after you give your sister the news."

"Aight. I'ma call her now."

"Bye."

I ended the call and went to my call log to find Paris's name, when there was a knock on my office door. I flipped around, and my backbone stiffened. "Mel? What are you doing here?" I asked, placing my phone on my desk.

"Can we talk?"

"We don't have shit to discuss," I informed her.

"You and I both know that's not true."

She closed the door behind her. "I'm sorry, Donny. I know the dinner was unexpected and awkward. You were the last person I expected to see that night."

"The feeling is mutual, Mel. I haven't seen you in over ten years, and now it's twice within a few weeks. Why are you here?"

Melanie sighed as her familiar scent of jasmine and vanilla hijacked the room. "Look, I knew Neema wouldn't be here today. That's the only reason I came."

"What do you mean?"

Mel's brown eyes hooked onto mine as we silently stared each other down. It had been almost a decade since she'd stepped foot inside the diner that she used to spend every waking moment at when we were growing up.

"When I kept pressing her about the *friend* she had a crush on, I didn't think it would be you, but looking back on it, I should've known," she stated, snapping me back to reality. "Are you two dating?"

"Hold up. You came here to talk to me about Neema?"

"What's up with you two? Are you serious?"

"Why is that any of your business?"

"It's not. I'm just trying to look out for you."

My brows compressed over my eyes as I scoffed. "Look out for me, how?"

"I started looking into her. At first, it was little things, like trying to find her on social media. Then, when I didn't find her there, I started Googling her."

"Why are you doing all this?"

"Because I don't know if she's who she says she is."

"I thought you were supposed to be her friend."

"And I thought you were supposed to be her boss," she responded.

My eyes rolled toward the ceiling. "Anything else, Mel?"

"That's all."

"Then, if you don't mind, I've got a business to run."

She folded her arms across her chest. "Yeah. Okay. It's clear it was a mistake coming here."

I pressed my lips into a hard line. "Yup."

"Just be careful. There are a lot of Neema Ellison's out there, but none of them are her."

I sucked my teeth. "We've lived in the same place our entire lives, and yet you haven't stepped foot in this diner since—" I paused. "And now I'm supposed to believe you wanna look out for me? I'm good, aight?"

"Yeah. Sure."

"You ran off and settled into your serene suburban life, and you're happy, right? You got everything you wanted?"

"Don—"

"Then do us both a favor and leave me in your rearview where I'm supposed to be, right along with *our* son."

Her eyes immediately shifted toward the floor. "Don, I—"

I shook my head, unwilling to hear anything she had to say. Our relationship would always be a staple in my memory, but how we ended shit would never sit right with me. Mel and I became inseparable the summer after eighth grade and stumbled into a relationship soon after. By junior year, we were both working at the diner, her waitressing and me flipping burgers in the back. She told me she was pregnant the night of our prom, and had I had it my way, I would've made her my wife right then and there. But she and her family had other plans. Having an abortion went against her religion, so we agreed she would carry the baby to full-term and consider giving it up for adoption. We kept her pregnancy a secret from everyone. She wore baggy clothes, took extra classes to finish school early, and went out of town to all her prenatal appointments.

The closer she got to delivering our son, the more I knew I didn't want to go along with the idea of a closed adoption. After begging and pleading with her to see things my way, I went to my parents with a proposition. Knowing how important family was to us, we planned to fight for custody and raise the baby independently. Two weeks before my son was born, my parents died in a tragic car accident, and since I was seventeen, I didn't have anyone legally willing to allow me to keep and raise my child. The day she delivered our son, her parents showed up with lawyers and paperwork, ready for us to sign over our rights to a local couple who'd been trying to conceive for six years. I hadn't told a soul that the biggest reason I was fighting so hard to save the diner was so that I had a reason to stick around and continue to watch him grow up from afar.

"Signing those papers was one of my biggest regrets," I mumbled.

"Don, I didn't come here to talk about that."

I scoffed. "You're so wrapped up in your perfect, shiny life that you can't even allow yourself to mention the baby you had with me? *Our* son? The one you and your parents pressured me to sign my rights away to and put up for adoption. God forbid we talk about any of that, right?"

A sob caught in her throat before she swallowed it down. "Will you just shut up about that? Everything we did back then was for a reason, okay? I'm sorry, but I can't live in the past like you do."

"I don't live there, but at least I can acknowledge that it happened, Mel. I mean, come on. It's like I'm staring at a stranger right now."

"You should be because I am not the scatter-brained seventeen-year-old girl you used to know, Donovan. I'm a married woman with goals and aspirations, and—"

"Kids? Two, right? I saw the family pictures in the hallway," I stated. "Twins, right? They're cute."

A pensive look stretched across her brown features. "What do you want from me?"

"I don't know. The truth... maybe an apology."

Her eyebrows collided above her button nose as she dabbed her eyes with the back of her hand. "An apology? For what? Because I won't apologize for having a good life or moving on and making something of myself. I was going through a lot back then, Donny. Making that decision broke me mentally and spiritually, and I had to learn how to rebuild myself from that loss. I won't apologize for how I chose to heal myself."

The baby was born over winter break during our senior year, and since Mel had worked so hard to complete a lot of her online classes ahead of time, she didn't have to return to school for the spring semester. She got accepted early into some fancy four-year college and got her diploma secretly without graduating with the rest of her class. Years later, she returned to the city and acted like I was just another face in the crowd.

"And what about what I lost? You *never* acknowledged my pain, Mel. My parents died two weeks before he was born. They never got to lay eyes on their grandchild, and then you up and sided with your family and those lawyers. No one's ever cut me deeper."

"I'm sorry, but getting pregnant and having a kid at seventeen? That wasn't my story, Donny. That wasn't *our* story. I knew you were hurting, but I just couldn't deal with your feelings on top of mine. It was too much, and I know I pushed you away."

"And I know I let you because I was tired of fighting everything and everyone. You were always the one person in my corner, and then you fucked around and... You know, what, never mind. I'm good."

"No, say it," she demanded as tears leaked from her eyes.

"Does your husband know?"

She shook her head. "No. He doesn't know about any of it, and I plan to keep it that way."

I scoffed. "Right."

"He's running for mayor, Donny. Our past needs to stay the past. Does she know?"

"Not the whole story."

"What did you say to her?"

"She felt the tension in the room and overheard a piece of our conversation in the hallway. So, on the ride home, I told her we used to date."

"And that's all?"

"That's all."

"If you can promise me our secret will remain between us, I'll try to ensure you get the funding you need to do whatever you want with this place."

"What? Are you serious?"

"I am."

"Why would you help me?"

"Winning this election is all Theo cares about, and I'm trying to get in front of any blip from my past that could taint his chances of that," she confessed.

"So this is really about helping yourself."

"Call it whatever you want. Do we have a deal that you'll continue to keep your mouth shut? If so, I'll ask Theo what strings he can pull to find you the money you need."

"If I'm even going to consider what you're saying, I need more than your word, Mel."

"I can't give you anything more than that. I meant what I said, Donny. I'll ask."

"How soon would he be able to make something happen?"

Her shoulders bobbed. "I don't know."

"I don't know how much time I have left, Mel. Whatever strings he's gonna pull, I need him to do it fast."

"Okay. I'll talk to him, and I'll be in touch."

"How? You don't have my number."

"Have you changed your number since high school?"

I dipped my eyes toward the floor. "Nah."

"Then I have your number," she said before walking out.

A few seconds after Mel left, my phone chimed, and a new email notification popped up on my screen. I distractedly clicked it, and my eyes widened.

"No they fuckin' didn't," I mumbled as my eyes scanned the email from left to right.

My fingers tapped Neema's name before my brain had a chance to reconsider. She picked up on the third ring. "How'd it go with your sister?"

"I didn't call," I answered, defeat plaguing my voice.

"Why not? What's wrong?"

"I just got an email from that hotel group saying they received buy-in from three out of four of the shareholders of the diner and are calling a meeting next week to finalize the paperwork."

"That's it? It's *over*?"

My body felt as if it were on fire as I scoffed. "Yup. It's over. Everyone is coming into town next week to sign on the dotted line and collect their fuckin' checks."

"Can't you refuse to sign or hold out?"

"Hold out for what? It's three against one now. I'm the only one that wants to keep this place, and I still *don't* have an angel investor."

My brother had been MIA for years, and in the blink of an eye, the tables turned, and there was nothing I could do about it.

"I'm so sorry. Is there anything I can do?"

"This is it. By next week, everyone in here will be out of a job, and

I'll be two hundred and fifty thousand dollars richer," I stated with zero enthusiasm in my tone.

I heard the shower water running in the background as Neema sighed into the receiver. "Don, I know you're upset right now."

Upset was an understatement. I felt defeated, played, and as useless as a three-dollar bill. "I'ma call you back. I just need a minute to process this shit, aight?"

"Yeah. Of course. I'm here if you need me," I heard Neema say before I ended the call.

* * *

I HAD BEEN DROWNING my sorrows in whiskey since the sun went down, when there was a knock at my apartment door. Drink in hand, I swung open the door to see Neema standing there with a fresh batch of homemade chocolate chip muffins in hand.

"Hi."

"H-hi," she mumbled.

"It's late. What are you..."

"The plan was to leave these on your doorstep, but you opened the door faster than I expected," she explained as a soft laugh sprang from her lips.

"Oh."

"I know you said you wanted to be alone. I just—"

I waved my hand to stop her. "I don't want to be alone anymore... ever. Please, come in."

"Are you sure?"

"Yes, Neema. I'm sure."

I stepped to the side and watched her hips sway as she sauntered past me wearing tight blue jeans. The enticing image of her firm curves and slender limbs squirming beneath my weight danced through my head. "Did you have a hard time sleeping tonight?"

"I tossed and turned, worrying about you. Hence, the muffins."

"Sounds like you needed me next to you."

She placed the plastic container on the kitchen counter. "It's been a long time since I shared a bed with someone. I'm equally terrified of sleeping alone as I am sleeping next to someone."

"You know you're always safe with me, right?"

Neema turned to face me with a ghost of a smile across her face. "You and those sweet words of yours."

"Did I say something wrong?"

"Not at all."

"Then what is it?"

She sighed before slowly deciding to make eye contact with me. "It's just, the word *safe* is kind of a trigger for me."

"In what way, if you don't mind me asking?"

"My life is heavy, Don. It's been that way all my life. When I was six, my birth mother committed suicide by hanging herself with an extension cord. After that, I was in and out of foster care until I aged out of the system. That was ten years ago, and being here... this is the first place I can say I feel *safe*," she said, a wry smile touching her lips.

I reached out to pull her into a tight hug. "As someone who doesn't let my walls down easily, I appreciate you for opening up to me," I assured her.

"Yeah, well, let me stop yapping before you have me spilling another secret of mine."

"Whatever secrets you're holding onto, know they're protected with me."

She smiled as if fine before boosting herself onto the edge of my kitchen counter and pulling her shirt over her head. "Now that I'm here... I don't think I want to talk anymore."

"What do you want to do then?" I asked before my body surged into hers.

I began nibbling her ears before placing my lips on hers. I peeled off her tight blue jeans, leaving her clad in only French-cut panties and a lace bra. I cupped her breasts while wrapping her thighs around my waist. The moonlight peeking through the kitchen window blinds cast a soft white glow against her brown skin as I penetrated her.

Nine

INDIGO

One week later.

I WAS WALKING downtown past the café Mel turned me onto a few weeks prior when I spotted her seated at a table near the window. We hadn't spoken since the dinner party, and I wasn't sure if there was a reason for her cold shoulder or if it was all in my head. Instead of jumping from one conclusion to the next, I allowed my legs to carry me inside to grab a coffee before going over to her table.

"Mel, hey." I greeted her with a brief wave.

She pressed the napkin to her lips before speaking. "Neema, hi. How are you?"

"I'm good. How are you?" I asked, looking around at the table. There was a jacket hung over the back of one of the chairs and a purse cradled in the seat beside her.

"I'm doing alright. I'm here with a couple of ladies from my home-owner's association. We're planning a neighborhood garage sale in the next couple of weeks," she explained.

"Listen, I'm sorry we left your party so unexpectedly. I wasn't feeling well."

She shook her head. "No. It's fine," she replied before stepping away from the table of ladies she was with.

"I reached out a couple times and didn't hear anything back, then I saw you canceled your last few yoga classes. Is everything okay?"

"Yeah. Everything is fine. I've just been busy, y'know, with Theo and the twins and everything."

"I don't think I've ever asked about your kids. How is it being a mom of more than one tiny human?"

She gave a breathless laugh before answering without making eye contact. "Taxing. Hey, um, can we try and catch up some other time? I'm a little busy now, and I should get my head wrapped around this garage sale. I would ask you to join, but I'm sure you've already got plans."

I wasn't sure if she knew I knew about her history with Don, but she was clearly uncomfortable around me and was doing a bad job hiding it.

"Um, yeah. Let's try and meet up again soon. I think I'm ready for my next one-on-one yoga session."

"Yeah. That sounds good."

"Cool. Well, I'll see you around."

"Hey, Neema, wait. I meant to ask, are you on social media? I tried looking you up on a couple of platforms and couldn't find a profile for you."

I felt the breath catch in my throat. Why the fuck was she looking into me? "No. I'm not," I answered with my head held high.

"Why not?" she inquired, head cocked to the side.

"Unlike a lot of my millennial counterparts, social media isn't my thing. Is me not being on social media an issue for you?"

"Of course not. Why would it be? I was just curious, that's all," she answered, lips tense around her words.

"Are you sure?"

She met my eyes and gave a nervous laugh. "Y-yeah. It's just, my husband's campaign manager is breathing down my neck about who I'm seen with around town, what I'm wearing, and what I'm doing every second of the day. Like, are you my dad, the fashion police, or what?"

"Sounds stressful."

She belted out another shaken laugh. "You don't know the half."

"So was it you or your husband's campaign manager that was curious about my absence on social media?"

"More him than me, really. Seriously, Neema, I was just curious."

I smiled with a touch of disdain. "It's cool. I'm just kidding around with you," I said as my phone rang. "I've got to take this. I'll let you get back to your meeting. Bye."

"Bye." She waved.

I pushed Mel's awkward vibes out of my head before pressing the phone to my ear and answering Don's call. "Hey, you."

"The signing is tomorrow morning at ten. Can you come?" he asked, bypassing a casual greeting.

I could hear the anxiety in his voice over the sizzle of food dropping in hot grease in the background. "Are you... in the kitchen?" I inquired.

"Yeah. Tony called out because his kid is sick, and Big L can't get in until he gets his kid on the bus, so it's just me handling the kitchen right now."

A smile stretched across my face. "A man that can cook. Hm. I guess you do learn something new every day."

"Back to the signing. Can you come?"

I sighed before sipping the bitter coffee I'd grabbed before leaving the café. The demons from my past had left my mind and body battered and bruised, but the feelings I felt for Don were so unexpected and dangerous that it felt like my heart could swell and burst at any second. I'd fallen in love with our connection and, in return, had been opening up more than anticipated. It was reckless, and I knew it, but that didn't stop me from enveloping him in all my thoughts and free time.

"Yeah," I finally spoke. "I'll come."

Don breathed a sigh of relief into the receiver when I accepted. "Thank you. It's been a long time since we've all been in the same room together. I need you there to make sure I don't murder all my siblings in cold blood. I ain't a killer but don't push me, ya dig?" he stated before a brief chuckle fell off his lips.

Amusement sat lightly on my face as I followed up with a laugh. "I got you."

"I have half a mind to fly and go anywhere but here, but I'ma chill."

"How long has it been?"

"About a year or so after our parents' accident."

"Sheesh. I think I'm more nervous than you are."

"Why?"

"I haven't been anyone's girlfriend in a long time. How welcoming have your siblings been to your exes?"

"They don't bite. My sisters might grill you. That's about it," Don assured me. "Besides, I haven't brought a girl around since high school."

"Let me guess, Mel?" I inquired.

"Yeah."

I cheesed, quickly trying to stop my brain from going down the rabbit hole of lies. "I bet you were popular with the ladies in high school, huh?"

"A lil." He answered modestly.

"Yeah, a lil heartbreaker."

"Chill."

"What's wrong? Can't stand the heat? Then you gotta get outta the kitchen," I teased.

"What about you? How many times have you been in love?"

"Too many."

"Care to share?"

"Not a chance. If you're looking for a romance novel, go find somebody else's story to listen to," I informed him.

"That's it, huh? Case closed?"

"For now," I answered. "Your sole focus needs to be on tomorrow."

Since we'd become official, I'd been toying with the idea of coming clean to Don about the broken pieces of my past, but I hadn't decided exactly when I'd drop the bomb. I wasn't ready for the dynamic between us to change.

He sighed. "You're right. We'll table the tales of Neema's love life for another time."

"Right. Another time."

* * *

MY EYES PINGED from the coffee table covered with tattered magazines on display to the receptionist's desk and back again as I waited alongside Don in the waiting room the next morning. We'd arrived twenty minutes early for the ten o'clock meeting, and no one else had come. We were led down the hallway to a conference room with plain-colored walls and rolling chairs around a boardroom-style table. I sat in the thin-padded seat next to Don while observing the freshly printed papers stacked next to a jar of black pens with the hotel group's logo printed on them and bottles of water in the center of the wooden table.

"How are you feeling?" I asked, glancing to my left.

"Better with you here," he replied before joining his hand with mine underneath the table. Don's nerves were visibly stretched taut as he awaited the arrival of his siblings.

"Hey, um, after this, do you think we could go somewhere and talk? There's something I want to tell you."

Don arched his right eyebrow. "Is it important?"

"Not more important than this. It can wait, trust me."

Before he could continue our conversation, the door opened, revealing two women standing behind one another.

"Why is she here?" his sister Paris snapped, aiming her index finger at me.

"Hello again to you, too," I responded dryly.

"Yo, chill, Paris. She's here because I asked her to be," Don said.

His other sister smiled. She was a few shades darker than Don, with a blonde buzz cut and a shiny diamond stud in her left nostril. "Excuse our rude ass older sister. Hi. I'm Destiny."

"Neema," I responded, returning a polite smile.

"So, Neema, how do you know my knuckleheaded little brother?" she quizzed.

"I'm a grown-ass man," Don interjected.

"I work at the diner, but we're..."

"We're together," he announced to his sisters.

"Together? Since when?" Paris quizzed.

"Let's not pretend that all of a sudden you care about my personal life."

Destiny turned her eyes to Don before leaning back in her chair. "Where's our brother?"

He scoffed. "Your guess is as good as mine."

Paris rolled her eyes. "He's always late."

Destiny belted out a soft chuckle. "Didn't Dad always used to tell him he'd be late to his own funeral?"

"He did," Don added.

Of their own accord, my eyes drifted to the wastebasket and over to the water cooler nestled in the corner of the room while the three of them strolled down memory lane. I jerked my eyes toward the door when it opened again. Fear shimmied up my bones, and my entire body ran cold. I immediately dropped my grip on Don's hand underneath the table while staring into the eyes of my *not so dead* husband.

"It's about time you got here," Paris fussed.

"Yeah. Sit down so we can get this over with," Destiny added.

Don twisted his neck toward me, and my body went tense with shock. "Neema, this is my half-brother, Enzo."

The ghost from my past stood in the doorframe with his vengeful brown eyes clamped onto mine. He snapped his eyes up from me before responding. "Sorry I'm late. Did you miss me?"

TO BE CONTINUED...

Afterword

A note from K.L. Hall.
    Reader,

Thank you for reading *Because You Don't Know My Name: A Potomac Falls Novella*. If you've made it this far, I hope you'll consider taking a minute to tell me what you thought about the book in the form of a **book review and/or rating**. Don't hesitate to let me know what you'd like to see from me next! I thoroughly enjoy reading your thoughts and hearing from you as well! I'm always striving to attract new readers and retain current ones, and reviews are one of the easiest ways to attract readers. If you loved the book, tell a friend, and most importantly, let me know!

All my love,
    K.L. Hall

K.L. Hall is a national bestselling and award-winning author. As a serial storyteller, Hall has penned over three dozen titles in various genres—including African American urban fiction and romance, paranormal, children's books (as Kimberley M.), and non-fiction. Her fictional stories straddle the intersection of classic Urban and spell-binding Romance.

Highly Acclaimed Titles:
In the Arms of a Savage: (Peaked at #1 in Women's Fiction)
The Potomac Falls Series (Peaked at #1 and #2 in African American Erotica)

Sign up for my mailing list to stay updated with new releases, giveaways, sneak peeks, and more! Click this link: https://bit.ly/38RMpV5

Connect with me on social media:

Facebook: https://www.facebook.com/authorklhall
Twitter: https://twitter.com/authorklhall
Instagram: https://www.instagram.com/officialklhall/
Website: https://www.authorklhall.com

Other novels by K.L. Hall:
Diary of a Hood Princess 1-3
Rise of a Street King: The Justice Silva Story *(Spin-Off to the Diary of a Hood Princess series)*
Broken Condoms and Promises 1-3
In the Arms of a Savage 1-3

Built for a Savage: Blaze and Camille's Love Story *(Spin-Off to the In the Arms of a Savage Series)*

A Ruthle$$ Love Story 1-3

Fallin' for the Alpha of the Streets 1-2

The Most Savage of Them All: The Wolfe Calloway Story *(Prequel to the In the Arms of a Savage Series)*

When a Gangsta Loves a Good Girl

Caught Between my Husband and a Hustler

The Illest Taboo 1-2

To the Only Thug I'll Ever Love

A Lover's Heist: Chief and Gianna's Love Story

A Lover's Heist II: Rome and Lira's Love Story

A Lover's Heist III: Baby and Skai's Love Story

Crushed Velvet & Cashmere

Crushed Velvet & Cashmere 2

<u>Entanglements</u>

Short Reads + Novellas:

Bi-Curious: An Erotic Tale

Bi-Curious 2: Tastes Like Candy

House of Cards 1-2

A Savage Calloway Christmas *(Christmas novella to the In the Arms of a Savage Series)*

Lovin' the Alpha of the Streets: A Valentine's Day Novella *(Valentine's Day novella to the Fallin' for the Alpha of the Streets Series)*

Awakened: A Paranormal Romance

As Long as You Stay Down

Solace in Seven

Solace II: The Final Cut

Something Bleu

Something Borrowed

Something New

The Knight Before Christmas: A Potomac Falls Short

I'll Be Home for Christmas: A Potomac Falls Short Book II

<u>Triggered: A Potomac Falls Novella</u>

Because You Don't Know My Name: A Potomac Falls Novella

Children's Books:
     Princess for Hire
     Princess Twinkle Toes & the Missing Magic Sneakers
     Little One, Change the World
     Adjust Your Crown: A Self-Love Coloring Book for Children of
Color

Non-Fiction:
     Authors are a Business: The Booked & Busy Course Mini Book

Thank You

Thanks for reading! If you enjoyed this book, please leave a review on Amazon and mark it as read on Goodreads. We hate errors but they do happen. If you catch any, please send them to us directly at blovepublica tions@gmail.com with ERRORS as the subject.

www.ingramcontent.com/pod-product-compliance
Lightning Source LLC
Chambersburg PA
CBHW071452130726
47997CB00006B/2333